SOPHOCLES

in an hour

BY CARL R. M

SUSAN C. MOORE, SERIES EDITOR

PLAYWRIGHTS in an hour
know the playwright, love the play

IN AN HOUR BOOKS • HANOVER, NEW HAMPSHIRE • INANHOURBOOKS.COM
AN IMPRINT OF SMITH AND KRAUS PUBLISHERS, INC • SMITHANDKRAUS.COM

*With grateful thanks to Carl R. Mueller, whose
fascinating introductions to his translations of the
Greek andGerman playwrights provided
inspiration for this series.*

Published by In an Hour Books
an imprint of Smith and Kraus, Inc.
177 Lyme Road, Hanover, NH 03755
inanhourbooks.com   SmithandKraus.com

Know the playwright, love the play.

In an Hour, In a Minute, and Theater IQ are registered trademarks of
In an Hour Books.

Front cover design by Dan Mehling, dmehling@gmail.com
Text design by Kate Mueller, Electric Dragon Productions
Book production by Dede Cummings Design, DCDesign@sover.net

ISBN-13: 978-1-936232-26-0
ISBN-10: 1-936232-26-X
Library of Congress Control Number: 2009943209

CONTENTS

Why Playwrights in an Hour?

This new series by Smith and Kraus Publishers titled Playwrights in an Hour has a dual purpose for being: one academic, the other general. For the general reader, this volume, as well as the many others in the series, offers in compact form the information needed for a basic understanding and appreciation of the works of each volume's featured playwright. Which is not to say that there don't exist volumes on end devoted to each playwright under consideration. But inasmuch as few are blessed with enough time to read the splendid scholarship that is available, a brief, highly focused accounting of the playwright's life and work is in order. The central feature of the series, a thirty- to forty-page essay, integrates the playwright into the context of his or her time and place. The volumes, though written to high standards of academic integrity, are accessible in style and approach to the general reader as well as to the student and, of course, to the theater professional and theatergoer. These books will serve for the brushing up of one's knowledge of a playwright's career, to the benefit of theater work or theatergoing. The Playwrights in an Hour series represents all periods of Western theater: Aeschylus to Shakespeare to Wedekind to Ibsen to Williams to Beckett, and on to the great contemporary playwrights who continue to offer joy and enlightenment to a grateful world.

Carl R. Mueller
School of Theater, Film and Television
Department of Theater
University of California, Los Angeles

Introduction

S ophocles was only twenty years younger than Aeschylus, but seems to have inhabited an entirely different world. "My dramatic wild oats were imitations of Aeschylus' pomp," Plutarch quotes him as saying, "then I evolved my own harsh mannerisms. And finally I embraced that style which is best, as most adapted to the portrayal of human nature."

During his long and reputedly untroubled life, Sophocles wrote over a hundred tragedies, of which only a precious seven survive, mostly from his middle and late periods. His abiding theme is human nature in relation to the universe.

The art scholar Margarete Bieber suggests we keep a contemporary statue of Sophocles in mind when trying to understand the Greek conception of the hero. In that statue, from the Beazley Archives, Sophocles appears gravely beautiful, expressing physical strength, and an ordered soul. But we should also keep his plays in mind, since they are among the most perfect and profound works of drama ever written. His quintessential tragic hero, unlike the uniform and solemn statue, is the man with a double nature, both blessed and cursed.

Typical of these is *Philoctetes*, whose hero, a wounded warrior of the Trojan War, has been isolated on an island because of his foul-smelling wound, but who possesses a magic bow necessary for the victory of the Greeks. (In *The Wound and the Bow,* Edmund Wilson made Philoctetes into the symbol of the modern artist, supremely gifted, yet proudly offensive.)

The same is true of Oedipus, especially in *Oedipus at Colonus*, where he is a blind old man, banished by humans and cursed by the gods, yet still capable of bestowing blessings on Athens before he dies.

On the surface, *Oedipus the King*, *Oedipus at Colonus*, and *Antigone* would seem to constitute a trilogy, since they all tell stories of the same family in a relatively consecutive fashion. But these three plays were written at separate stages in the playwright's career, and they are not always factually or chronologically consistent. In *Oedipus the King,* for example, Oedipus banishes himself from Thebes. In *Oedipus at Colonus,* written twenty-five years later, about a year before the playwright's death, Oedipus claims he was banished by Creon. Similarly, *Antigone,* though historically the last play in the Oedipus cycle, was actually written first.

Another important facet of Sophocles' theater is the way that he humanizes Attic tragedy, which was normally a religious expression exalting the power of the gods. While clearly a religious man, Sophocles dramatically reduces the role of the Olympian gods and goddesses in his plays. For one thing, the gods rarely appear on stage. That is why the role of prophecies and oracles, the human instruments of the gods, grows exponentially more important.

While Sophocles remains supreme in his capacity to dramatize angry, argumentative encounters —between, say, Antigone and Creon, or between Oedipus and Tiresias — he is best remembered for the perfection of the tragic art, which is why he was so clearly Aristotle's favorite playwright, and the model for neo-classicists ever after. In *Oedipus the King,* Sophocles created what may very well be the most perfectly plotted play ever composed. And while Aeschylus was often inchoate and obscure, Sophocles is always clear and melodious, writing dramatic verse that almost hums, which is why his contemporaries called him "The Bee."

Robert Brustein
Founding director of the Yale and American Repertory Theatres,
Distinguished Scholar in Residence, Suffolk University

Sophocles

IN A MINUTE

AGE YEAR (BCE)

AGE	YEAR	
–	500	Thespis creates Greek Tragedy for the Great Dionysia.
–	499	Aeschylus's first tragedy performed at Athens City Dionysia.
–	**496**	**Enter Sophocles.**
6	490	Persian Wars begin with Greek victory at Marathon.
16	480	The Persian fleet is defeated at Salamis by the Greek fleet commanded by Themistocles.
17	479	Greece becomes a direct democracy and initiates trial by jury.
20	476	Phrynichus's play *Phoenician Women* is controversial in that it deals with the past.
24	472	Aeschylus's *Persians* describes the battle of Salamis.
26	470	Aeschylus adds a second character to the cast of Greek drama — a major innovation.
28	**468**	***Triptolemus* wins Sophocles his initial first prize at the Athens Dionysia.**
34	462	Athens's soldiers and judges become salaried employees of the state.
35	461	Pericles takes power in Athens, initiating a golden age for Greek culture.
36	460	Aeschylus's *Prometheus Bound* plays to full houses.
38	**458**	**Sophocles adds a third actor. Aeschylus adopts this and wins first prize for his *Oresteia Trilogy*.**
41	455	Euripides enters the Dionysia for the first time with *Daughters of Pelias,* which wins third prize.
46	450	Greece has 2 million citizens and 1 million slaves. Athens has 50,000 citizens, 100,000 slaves.
47	449	The Greeks sign a peace treaty with the Persian ruler Xerxes I.
53	**443**	**Sophocles' *Antigone* wins drama critics' award.**
65	431	The Peloponnesian War begins, pitting Athens against Sparta for Greek dominance.
66	430	A devastating plague breaks out in Athens.
67	429	Enter Plato.
71	425	Aristophanes' *Acharnians* wins first prize in a new category, comedy.
?	**?**	**Sophocles' *Electra, Oedipus the King, Ajax,* and *Women of Trachis* are produced, dates unknown.**
75	421	Greece and Sparta sign peace of Nicias — for a short-lived six years.
76	420	Euripides' *Electra*
85	411	"Oligarchs" overthrow Athenian democracy — for a short-lived three years.
87	**409**	**Sophocles' *Philoctetes* wins first prize at the Athens Dionysia.**
90	**406**	**Exit Sophocles.**
–	**401**	**Sophocles' *Oedipus at Colonus* is produced by his grandson and wins first prize at the Dionysia.**
–	399	Socrates is tried and executed in Athens.

In one minute or less, this section gives you a snapshot of the playwright's world. From historical events to the literary landscape of the time, this brief list catalogues events that directly or indirectly impacted the playwright's writing.

Sophocles

HIS WORKS

All caps indicate an existing play.

DRAMATIC WORKS
Dates Known
AJAX [ca. 444]
ANTIGONE [ca. 442]
ELECTRA [ca. 424–421]
OEDIPUS AT COLONUS [ca. 406]
OEDIPUS THE KING [ca. 424–421]
PHILOCTETES [ca. 409]
Triptolemus [ca. 468]
WOMEN OF TRACHIS [ca. 424–421]

Dates Unknown
Crisis
Eurypylus
Gathering of the Acheans
Ichneutai
Inachus
Nausica
Phaedra
Skyrians
Telephia
Tereus
Thamyris

This section presents a complete list of the playwright's works.

Onstage with Sophocles

Introducing Colleagues and
Contemporaries of Sophocles

 ## THEATER

Aeschylus, Athenian tragic playwright [525–456]

Aristophanes, Athenian comic playwright [ca. 448–380]

Crates, Athenian Old Comedy playwright [ca. mid 5th c.]

Cratinus, Athenian Old Comedy playwright [ca. 520–423]

Epicharmus, Sicilian Greek comic poet [ca. 540–450]

Euripides, Athenian tragic playwright [ca. 480–406]

Phrynichus, Greek tragic playwright [ca. 511–476]

Pratinas, introduced satyr play to Athens [ca. late 6th–early 5th c.]

Sophron, Syracusan writer of mimes [ca. 5th c.]

Thespis, Greek actor and playwright [ca. 6th c.]

 ## ARTS

Micon, Greek painter [ca. mid 5th c.]

Phidias, Greek sculptor [ca. 480–ca. 430]

Polyclitus, Greek sculptor [ca. 450–420]

Polygnotus, Greek painter [ca. 500–440]

Pythagoras, Greek music theorist [ca. 570–ca. 495]

 ## POLITICS/MILITARY

Agesilaus II, king of Sparta [ca. 444–360]

Alcibiades, Athenian general and politician [ca. 450–404]

Aristides, founded Delian League [ca. 530–468]

This section lists contemporaries whom the playwright may or may not have known. Since fewer notables are known from the Classical Period, we have included some who predated the playwright.

Artaxerxes, king of Persia [ca. 5th c.]

Cimon of Athens, Athenian statesman [ca. 510–450]

Cyrus the Younger, Persian prince and general [ca. 5th c.]

Darius I, king of Persia [ca. 549–486]

Darius II, king of Persia [ca. 5th c.–404]

Herodotus, Greek historian [ca. 484–ca. 425]

Mardonius, Persian military commander [ca. 5th c.–479]

Nicias, Athenian statesman and general [ca. 469–413]

Pericles, Athenian statesman and general [ca. 495–429]

Pisistratus, Athenian tyrant [ca. 6th c.–527]

Themistocles, Athenian statesman and general [ca. 524–459]

Thucydides, Greek historian [ca. 460–ca. 395]

Xenophon, Athenian soldier [ca. 430–354]

Xerxes I, king of Persia [ca. 520–465]

Xerxes II, king of Persia [ca. 5th c.]

SCIENCE

Alcmaeon of Croton, Natural philosopher [ca. 6th c.]

Hippocrates, Greek physician [ca. 460–ca. 370]

Ictinus, designed rebuilding of the Athenian Acropolis
[ca. mid 5th c.]

Callicrates, designed rebuilding of the Athenian Acropolis
[ca. mid 5th c.]

Protagoras, Greek mathematician and philosopher [ca. 490–420]

Susrata, Indian surgeon [ca. 6th c.]

LITERATURE

Aesop, Greek fable writer [ca. 620–560]

Anacreon, Greek poet [ca. 570–ca. 488]

Bacchylides, Greek poet [ca. 507–ca. 450]

Pindar, Greek composer and poet [ca. 522–443]

Simonides of Ceos, Greek poet [ca. 556–468]

RELIGION/PHILOSOPHY

Anaxagoras, Greek philosopher from Asia Minor [ca. 500–428]

Confucius, Chinese philosopher [ca. 551–479]

Democritus, Greek philosopher [ca. 460–ca. 370]

Empedocles, Greek philosopher [ca. 490–430]

Ezra, Hebrew scribe [ca. 5th c.]

Heraclitus, Greek philosopher [ca. 535?–475?]

Meh-Ti, Chinese philosopher [ca. 5th c.]

Mo-tzu, Chinese Philosopher [ca. 470–391]

Parmenides, Greek philosopher [ca. early 5th c.]

Plato, Greek philosopher [ca. 428–348]

Siddhartha Gautama, the Buddha, founder of Buddhism,
    [ca. 563–483]

Socrates, Greek philosopher [ca. 470–399]

Xenophanes, Greek philosopher [ca. 570–480]

SOPHOCLES

in an
hour

BEGINNINGS

Sophocles lived during most of the fifth century BCE, the century commonly known as the Golden Age of Athens. He was born most likely in 496, and he died in 406. The son of a wealthy Athenian, Sophilus, Sophocles was good-looking, cultivated, and accomplished. He was born in Colonus Hippos, a rural district north of Athens, which today is a rundown section of Athens near a railroad terminal. It was in Colonus Hippos that Sophocles set the site of his final play, *Oedipus at Colonus*.

THE TIMES

In the early days of the fifth century, Athens, and Greece in general, were at great risk of invasion by the Persian Empire. The Persian-Greek conflict started with the support of mainland Greeks for the revolt of Asiatic Greeks against Persian domination. Persia already ruled European Greek territory in Thrace and Macedonia. Unfortunately, Persia

This is the core of the book. The essay places the playwright in the context of his world and analyzes the influences and inspirations within that world.

1

believed that there would be no security for itself as long as any Greek state remained independent. Although the threat of Persian domination began as early as 514, the first major battle was fought in 490 at Marathon, on the northeast coast of Attica. It was here that ten thousand Athenians and their allies met a Persian force of double that number. Although expected Spartan Greek reinforcements never showed up, Grecian armies routed the Persians. Aeschylus, the first of the great Athenian dramatists, fought in that battle at the age of thirty-five.

The second, and decisive, encounter was fought in 480 at Salamis, an island in the Saronic Gulf off the western coast of Attica. At Salamis the Greek fleet thoroughly defeated the Persian fleet, forcing it to withdraw to its home base in Asia Minor. It was not until 479 at Plataea that the Persians were finally driven from the Greek mainland. It was during the ceremonial celebration of that victory in Athens that a gloriously naked sixteen-year-old Sophocles marched, playing the pipes, as the chosen representative of the youth of Athens.

PEACE AND PROSPERITY

With these two astonishing victories, Greece achieved a half-century of comparative peace and unparalleled prosperity. In Athens, a society and state developed that has been the wonder of the world ever since. The foundations of a democratic state had been established in the previous century. In Athens, a democracy run directly by its adult male citizens took hold. It was the beginning of democracy. The term is based on the Greek words the rule (*kratos*) of the people (*demos*). This highly cherished right meant that every male Athenian citizen was directly involved in the governance of the state.

THE BEGINNINGS OF ATHENIAN TRAGEDY

Around 550, Thespis is said to have introduced the first speaker to step out of the Greek chorus. Although dates are not entirely certain, this is the time of the orchestra in the Agora at Athens. Around the same time, an area sacred to Dionysus was established on the south side of the hill of the Acropolis. In 534, Pisistratus introduced drama into the state festivals of Athens. Then around 500, the site of dramatic performance was moved from the Agora to the Precinct of Dionysus, where it remained. It was here that Greek drama evolved through numerous structural transformations.

THE LIFE AND WORK

Sophocles' life was as remarkable in length as it was in productivity. His first dramatic competition, in 468, was against Aeschylus; his last was in the City Dionysia in 406. The first was ten years before Aeschylus's death; the last a commemoration of the recent death of Euripides in 406. His own death followed shortly after.

It is estimated that Sophocles, dramatic output exceeded 120 plays. At least twenty won first prize, and eighteen were performed at the Great or City Dionysia in Athens. But Sophocles was more than a playwright. Like every male Athenian citizen, he was vitally involved in the governance of his city-state. During his fifties, he served as a general during the revolt of Samos, in 441–440, with his great friend the Athenian politician Pericles. Sophocles was so renowned that after his death he was rewarded with the honor of a hero cult. In ancient Greek religion, gods and heroes were worshipped.

Of his 120 plays only seven survive. Of those only two are positively dated: the *Philoctetes* in 409 and the *Oedipus at Colonus* in 406. *Oedipus at Colonus* was produced after his death by his grandson. Sophocles had several victories in 447 and 438, as well as with *Antigone* at an unknown date. The dates for *Ajax*, *Oedipus the King*, *Electra*, and *The Women of Trachis* are unknown. Earlier in the twentieth century, Sophocles was considered to be "stable, harmonious, and at ease with experience," as *The Oxford Classical Dictionary* (1996) reports, and it may well be true. Nonetheless, his plays have many examples of violence, discomfort, pain, and mental anguish. All of these are aspects of the vital theatricality that earlier times denied him. Critics from the early twentieth century simply did not want to recognize these difficult scenes. John Gould speaks of Sophocles as "the master of the enacted metaphor — metaphors of blindness in the two *Oedipus* plays and *Antigone*, of bestiality in *Trachiniae* — which is momentarily 'realized' in the text as it is performed. The theatricality of such pervasive dramatic metaphors emerges in moments such as the messenger speech of *Oedipus the King* and the immediately following scene with the entry of the now blinded but 'seeing' Oedipus . . ." One wonders at the perception of earlier critics who called Sophocles' drama "middling." There are few more powerful, more dramatic and theatrical moments in the history of world theater than those found in his plays.

RICH IN THEATRICALITY

The plays of Sophocles are rich in theatricality. Consider the prologue of the play *Ajax*. Athena's voice is heard seemingly from nowhere, while Odysseus looks for traces of Ajax's tracks in the sandy soil of the beach outside Ajax's hut. Odysseus looks around in the early morning fog to find the voice that only takes on bodily form eventually as it emerges from the mist. Or call to mind the "baiting game" that Athena plays with Odysseus in the same play. She leads him by the proverbial nose. She is condescending in tone and arch in attitude. Athena makes the most of his fear of being exposed to the "raving" Ajax inside his hut. And when she finally coaxes Ajax out of his dwelling, she manipulates Odysseus like a puppet at the end of her strings. These are moments of brilliant theatricality. Like any master dramatic creator, Sophocles gives us not the expected but the unexpected possibility.

There are many other purely functional aspects of Sophocles' plays that he transforms into theatrical gold. One of them has to do with the theatrical prop. In *Electra*, Sophocles plays a wonderfully extended theatrical "game" with what must be considered one of the major props in any of his plays: the funeral urn that ostensibly contains Orestes' ashes. Electra is told the false tale that her brother Orestes died in the Pythian Games at Delphi (to hide his actual presence). She is given the funeral urn containing his ashes. From that moment forward, she cannot be parted from the urn that she thinks contains the last remains of her beloved brother. After all, she once saved him from destruction, and he was to be the avenger of their father, Agamemnon's, murder. All that she held dear — her hopes, her love, her expectations — is now in that urn. She grieves and laments inconsolably over it. Even when Orestes tries to reveal himself to Electra and take the urn from her, she refuses to let go of it. The brilliant use of this central prop is in the presence onstage of the living Orestes throughout her lamentation. Gould's succinct summation of this coup-de-théâtre is apropos: "The fusing of game-playing, irony, and intensity of tragic emotion is mediated through the simple 'prop.'" Other major examples of theatrically conceived props in Sophocles are the sword in *Ajax*, the gift of his enemy, the Trojan Hector, with which Ajax will kill himself; and the magically endowed bow of Heracles in *Philoctetes*, without which the Trojan War will not be won by the Greeks.

ENTRANCES AND EXITS

Given the presumed layout of the Greek theater of Sophocles' time, entrances and exits are endowed with particular theatrical power and effectiveness. This is true even though we don't know exactly how the space was configured. The blinded Oedipus enters through the main doors of the palace immediately following one of the greatest messenger speeches in Greek tragedy. The entrance is nothing less than shattering in its effect. Its near equal is the final entrance of Creon in *Antigone*. Creon's wife, Eurydice, exits silently after learning of the death of her son Haemon. Creon enters carrying the body of that son. Almost immediately following Creon's entrance, the Messenger reenters with news of Eurydice's suicide. This is followed by the immediate appearance of her dead body. It is pushed out through the central doors on the scenic device known as the *ekkyklêma*, a platform on wheels to "reveal" a sight inside the house. The rapid juxtaposition of these moments of destruction and devastation are the work of a master poet of the theater. If it is Sophocles' intention to repay Creon for his unbending stubbornness that caused the deaths of the three people closest to him, then he has done so with brilliant theatricality. These are only a few of many examples, the last of which are to be found in *Philoctetes*. Here the hero's initial entrance onto the scene is announced by his groans and laments from afar, striking fear into the hearts of the Chorus of Sailors. His exit from Lemnos is equally dramatic. It is four times attempted, four times aborted. And it is realized only at the fifth attempt — having created great tension in the process.

NARRATIVE SPEECHES

Sophocles is also a master of the narrative speech. This speech is usually, but not always, delivered by a messenger. The descriptions of the death of Jocasta and the blinding of Oedipus are the most theatrically effective in all of Greek tragedy. Certainly no less moving, though of a different tone altogether, is the speech describing the death and apotheosis of the aged Oedipus in the sacred grove of the goddesses at Colonus. In *Electra*, the Tutor of Orestes narrates to Electra a description of the chariot race at the Pythian Games in Delphi during which Orestes is supposed to have been killed. To some this speech is excessively long, tedious, and adds nothing to the story. What this point of view fails to consider is that it is not the story narrated in the speech that is the main object of the narration. It is the effect that the speech has on the person it most directly concerns, namely Electra. Electra's entire world is annihilated during that speech so that she would welcome death in order to be reunited with the brother she loves.

But not only Electra is affected; so, too, is the audience. The spectator, after all, knows that not only is Orestes present to revenge his father's murder but he also sees the narration for the sheer fabrication that it is. Thus a grand expectation of the spectator is created in anticipation of the moment when Electra will know the truth. This moment of expectation is so great that Sophocles was inspired to write a scene of such ecstatic dimension that it could only be rendered in song. With this understanding in place, the false narration of Orestes' death becomes central to the theatrical structure of *Electra*, as well as the major irony. As we will discuss, it is probable that the Chorus "acted out" these narrative speeches.

IMPORTANCE OF PLACE

Place is an important playwriting asset that Sophocles never fails to use to great advantage. Ideally the dramatic action of a play occurs in the one place where it can logically happen, no other place being possible. Each of Sophocles' extant works observes this rule. Even so, his most successful applications of place are found in *Philoctetes* and in *Oedipus at Colonus*. In *Philoctetes*, the deserted island of Lemnos is clearly the logical location. But Sophocles, master craftsman that he is, makes metaphoric connections between the play's hero and the setting.

In *Oedipus at Colonus* the sacred precinct of the goddesses is put to sublime use onstage. The ancient, blind, and ragged Oedipus enters unknowingly upon this ground. This is a divinely inspired event. Antigone increases the mystery of its sanctity when she describes its heavenly peace and beauty. The citizens of Colonus frantically attempt to remove Oedipus from this sacred ground, unsuccessfully at first. Then they are successful through persuasion. The very length of this confrontation, all having to do with the place's holiness, is an example of highly effective, masterly stagecraft.

SCENES OF RECOGNITION

Surely the most distinctive aspect of Sophocles' dramaturgy is the idea of recognition. This is a factor little found in Aeschylus and Euripides, but it was considered by Aristotle as an essential of tragedy. It was at the center of Sophocles' view of existence. No play of Sophocles is without its central recognition scene. This is a scene in which "one or more characters realizes that he or she has misperceived the nature of reality and the realization is almost always associated with pain, suffering, and death," as Gould has pointed out. These misperceived communications are not only between humans but also between humans and gods. The communications between humans and gods come via oracles, dreams, and prophets. And these are almost always either false or so clouded in ambiguity that they invite misunderstanding. They are often a preamble to destruction.

Cedric Whitman calls this syndrome in the Sophoclean scheme of things "late learning." Both Deianira and Heracles in *The Women of Trachis* understand too late the nature and meaning of oracles. They learn the truth only after the action is taken and the tragic fall into chaos and death has been set in motion. In *Ajax* an accurate understanding of Athena's intention comes too late to prevent the tragic death of Ajax — and so too in the other five plays of Sophocles. "Learning too late," writes Whitman, "is nothing new in Greek poetry."

THE GREEK THEATER AND ITS STRUCTURE

When we think of the structure of the Greek theater in antiquity, the first image that comes to mind is the "traditional" one of a *skênê*, a building that served as a background to the action. The building had from one to three doors in it. In front of it, there was a circular acting area made of pounded earth circled in stone, known as the orchestra. But modern scholarship has questioned that conventional image. One aspect of the Greek theater is more than fairly certain: from its beginnings, Greek theater has had a very strong visual component.

Antiquity was constantly modifying and rebuilding its theater structures. This was true to such a degree that it is impossible to know what the theater space in Athens consisted of during the period of the fifth-century Classical dramatists. There is no evidence for the circular orchestra prior to 330 in the theater at Epidaurus. This theater was famous for its graceful symmetry and beauty. As for the Theater of Dionysus in Athens in the fifth century, it is possible to conceive of a much larger and more elaborate version of the tiny provincial theaters at Thorikos and Trachones in Attica. This would mean that in the Theater of Dionysus in the fifth century the audience would have been seated on wooden benches in a rectilinear arrangement close to the acting area. The acting area may have been loosely rectilinear or possibly trapezoidal, with only two parallel sides.

In any event, at the time of Sophocles, the central focal point was the orchestra, a flat space of pounded earth on which the Chorus sang and danced. Where the action itself of Athenian tragic theater in the fifth century took place is not known, as archeological evidence is lacking. Most likely the action was at the orchestra level. Or there might have been a low wooden platform (at most) in front of the *skênê*, or building, and a small flight of steps leading into the orchestra. Later in the century a row of columns was added to the front of the *skênê*. In any event, the architectural history of the Theater of Dionysus in Athens beginning in the latter part of the sixth century is much debated. What cannot be argued, however, is that during the time of the great Classical dramatists its architecture remained simple and undeveloped.

The stage and stage building (*skênê*) were most likely wooden and rebuilt each year for the performance. As Richard Green points out, vase paintings from the late fifth and early fourth centuries suggest that "the stage [of this period] was about a metre high [forty inches] with a flight of steps in the center communicating with the orchestra." In the *skênê*, which could represent numerous scenes, were a maximum of three doors, the central one for major entrances and exits, the two flanking ones for less important comings and goings. The building was used to represent a palace in *Oedipus the King*, a tent or hut in *Ajax*, a temple in *Iphigenia in Tauris*, a cave in *Philoctetes*, and the Brazen Threshold of Earth in *Oedipus at Colonus*. Clearly it was versatile.

Behind the central door was housed the *ekkyklêma*. This was a wheeled platform device measuring about 5 feet by a little more than 8 feet. It could be rolled out onto the stage to display scenes, most often of carnage, such as the bodies of the murdered Agamemnon and Cassandra; the inside of Ajax's hut with scores of slaughtered cattle surrounding him; and Oedipus, lying on the platform after his self-blinding. At the right edge of the stage was a machine used to lift gods and heroes onto the stage, or fly them off. This device was used only once by Sophocles. The roof of the building was available for the appearance of gods. (It had been used by mortals as late as the mid-fifth century, such as the Watchman in the opening of Aeschylus's *Agamemnon*.) To quote Richard Green once more: "The contrast between the hidden interior of the stage building and the daylight outside, between gods on high and the actors onstage, and between these and the chorus, half-way to the audience and virtually within its territory, are all physical facts which the playwrights exploited." It was not until 350–330 that Lycurgus gave Athens the Theater of Dionysus. This is the theater that is generally called to mind when imagining Athenian tragedy. It is a gleaming theater of stone: stone *skênê*, stone stoa, and stone auditorium built into the southern slope of the hill of the Acropolis. It is worth keeping in mind that this was not the theater of Sophocles' day.

STAGING TRADITION

Fifth-century staging tradition in the age of Sophocles is difficult to decipher. There are many vase paintings that almost certainly deal with stage representations of the myths that served as the basis of the tragedies. However, these images may exceed what was actually seen onstage. We are fairly certain that costumes were rich, elaborate, and formal. This is true, for example, on the Pronomos vase, an artifact dating from the end of the fifth century. It depicts a satyr play, but it shows costumes that could very well have been worn by characters in tragedies performed in the second half of the fifth century.

THE THEATER FESTIVALS OF ATHENS

What we know about production is essentially confined to plays mounted in Attica, even though other regions were active as well. In any event, from the close of the sixth and throughout the fifth century, tragedy was primarily performed as part of the Great or City Dionysia in Athens. Tragedy was also a part of the Lenaea festival during the winter months, when access to Athens was inhibited because of weather. But tragedy was not the sole reason for these festivals. They also scheduled processions, sacrifices in the theater, libations, the parade of war orphans, and the performance of dithyramb poems and comedy. The final day was devoted to a review of the conduct of the festival and to the awarding of prizes.

A festival would see three tragedians compete with three plays plus a satyr play each. The contestants and plays were chosen by the archon. He was a state official who also appointed three *chorêgoi*, who were responsible for the expense of equipping and training the choruses. The actors and playwrights were paid by the state. One representative from each of the ten tribes of Athens was chosen to judge the competition. The winning playwright was crowned with a wreath of ivy. Until the middle of the fifth century, the three tragedies of each day's performance comprised a trilogy. Eventually each of the plays featured a different subject. Thus Sophocles' tragedies were most often independent plays.

THE CHORUS

Of all the elements of Greek theatrical practice, the importance of the chorus cannot be overestimated. It was, after all, the major financial responsibility of the *chorêgoi*. Athens had a tradition of tragic dithyramb chorus competitions in both song and dance. It existed long before and well into the era of tragic theater. In Aeschylus's day the chorus numbered twelve. Sophocles added three. In *Tragedy in Athens*, Wiles convincingly argues that the choreography of the chorus was not in straight lines or highly formalized, as previously thought. Instead it was dynamically active. The split chorus in Sophocles' *Ajax*, for examples, enters through both side entrances searching for Ajax. They are agitated and most likely in a physically disordered state (choreographed disorder, to be sure). And when the Chorus of Old Men enters for the first time in *Oedipus at Colonus*, they, too, are highly agitated, as their text clearly indicates. They dart wildly about the orchestra in search of an intruder into the Sacred Grove. Finally, Wiles makes a most insightful deduction. He suggests that the subject of each choral ode is acted out by the chorus in choreographed dance. Even more startling, during long narrative speeches, the chorus was performing a choreography that visually complemented the verbal narration. This was probably true of the Messenger's speech describing Oedipus's self-blinding, and Eurydice's death scene in *Antigone*. One might also add the Tutor's narrative of Orestes' fictitious "death" at Delphi in Sophocles' *Electra*. The brilliance of this deduction is staggering: they were seldom inactive. They not only wore the persona of elders or of women friends of Electra but they also performed the contexts of other actors' narrations. This explains why Athenians who attended theater at festival times spoke of going to the "choreography" rather than to the play.

THE MASK

Critical to the staging of fifth-century Greek tragedy is the use of the mask. There is ample evidence of the use of masks in cult ceremonies, such as the grotesque mask worn in adolescent rites of passage in Sparta and the animal masks used in the cult of Demeter and Despoina at Lycosura. Closer to home are the masks worn in the cult of Dionysus, from which the mask in Greek tragedy likely derives. It is possible that the theatrical mask amplified the voice of the actor to reach, in some theaters, thousands of spectators. In any case, the dramatic mask is depicted from the fifth century onwards. Made generally of linen, the mask covered the entire head. In fifth-century tragedy, it was basically naturalistic and represented types rather than individuals.

The mask was essential to Athenian tragedy. It was practical to limit the number of speaking parts, and therefore masks, in any one scene to three actors. Patricia Easterling suggests the limit allowed the audience to know "where each voice is coming from," as facial movements were obscured by the masks. In addition to typing, masks permitted an actor to be cast in multiple roles. This offered financial benefits, as actors could be double- and perhaps even triple-cast. This practice is still much appreciated by contemporary theatrical producers. And alas, masks also helped deny women a place on the tragic stage by hiding the faces of the men who played all the parts. As for the numbers of nonspeaking actors onstage there was no limit, and exciting stage effects with scores of "extras" would not have been unusual. It was Sophocles who introduced a third actor, and thereby a third mask, to Greek theater. By doing this, he created a potential for considerably more complex scenes than those with the previously traditional two actors.

MUSIC IN TRAGEDY

Little is known about music in Archaic and Classical Greece. Some scores survive, but most are fragmentary and date from the Hellenistic period. Although the Greeks were knowledgeable about a great many musical instruments, they adopted only two main sorts: a stringed instrument (lyre) and a wind instrument or pipe (*aulos*). It was not a flute but sounded with a reed (single and double). In tragedy of the fifth century the double-pipe *aulos* was the instrument of choice to accompany the musical sections of the dramatic action.

The musical element in the performance of fifth-century tragedy was of primary importance. It was somewhat similar to modern opera. Each of the extant tragedies features short choral sections (usually five) during which the singing and dancing chorus commands center stage. In addition, there are sections in which song is exchanged between characters. Sometimes there is an alternation between spoken dialogue and song, the latter often between a character or characters and the chorus. Easterling rightly points out that these sections exist in the same time frame as the scenes of exclusively spoken dialogue. They are designed "to intensify emotion or to give a scene a ritual dimension, as in a shared lament or song of celebration." Solo singing became increasingly popular in Greek tragedy, with the plays of Euripides often topping the charts.

WHAT TO DO WITH THE AUDIENCE

There were two constants in Greek theater. These were open-air events centered around a clear area within which the chorus danced. Furthermore, the performance took place in the full light of day, endowing it with a visible reference, namely the audience. The audience was right there, not hidden in a darkened auditorium, and therefore had to be dealt with, unlike modern audiences.

With this as a given, playwrights went to great lengths to integrate the spectator into the performance. Sophocles in particular created strong bonds between the audience and the chorus, which was almost always present onstage. In Sophocles, plays the chorus becomes the audience's onstage extension. This illustrates the communal nature of the experience of Greek tragedy.

ACTING STYLE

A theater as enormous as the one used by Sophocles precluded an intimate acting style, though the spectators seldom tired of intimate subjects. The great size of the seating area, which held thousands of spectators, necessarily demanded an unabashedly extroverted performance. Gestures had to be exaggerated to be visible to the multitudes occupying the bleacher seats. Otherwise they might be misinterpreted. The need to reach out also benefited greatly from the bold masks that completely enveloped the actors' heads.

THEMES

Fifth-century Greek tragedy looked to the heroic past for themes. It drew on the *Iliad* and *Odyssey*. It also borrowed from tales from archaic times for its themes. Since Athens was part of Attica, the heroes of Attic tragedy are drawn from figures in Attic cults. Theseus, Heracles, and Oedipus became heroes in the plays of Sophocles.

TRAGEDY AND POLITICS IN TANDEM

Athenian political activity was a major element in Athenian tragedy. Many of the surviving plays of fifth-century Athens mirror its thriving political life. Critics have recently stressed the ideological and educational content of tragedy. They see vital connections between various aspects of tragic discourse and discourse in the legislative body of the Athenian assembly and the Athenian courts of law. In Sophocles' *Electra* we find a vivid example of how the rhetoric and discourse of the body politic may have influenced the scene in which Electra and Clytemnestra first meet. This is a scene that could easily have taken place opposite the Acropolis or be seen today on *Court TV.*

AJAX

Sophocles' first play, *Ajax*, is based on a rich and extensive literary tradition that includes a variety of tales and legends concerning its hero. Ajax figures in Homer's *Iliad*, where he is referred to repeatedly as of formidable stature, towering head and shoulders over every other Greek at Troy. He is spoken of as the greatest of the Greek heroes after Achilles. He is also a frequent point of reference in the odes of the fifth-century lyric poet Pindar.

The Ajax of legend is a figure very close and dear to the Athenian heart. His ancient kingdom was the island of Salamis just off the west coast of Attica. In the sixth century, during the age of Solon and Pisistratus, this island became an Athenian possession. Ajax is proudly referred to by Classical Athenians as the "bulwark of Athens." A very late example of his almost sacred connection to that city is the dedication of a Phoenician ship to him at Salamis. This ship was from the spoils of the great victory over the Persians at Salamis in 480.

Ajax is known to have been extraordinarily headstrong and self-centered. It is in that guise that we meet him in Sophocles' play. With the death of Achilles, as legend has it, the armor of that hero was to be awarded to the most worthy of the Greek heroes who survived him. The armor had been made by Hepheastus, the god of fire and metal-working. Given his reputation as the greatest hero after Achilles, Ajax had good reason to expect it. He was thwarted, however, when Greek leadership awarded it to Odysseus.

In his rage, Ajax decides to take revenge by murdering the generals Agamemnon and Menelaus, as well as his archrival Odysseus. But Athena steps in and scrambles Ajax's mind. This causes him instead, in the dead of night, to descend on the cattle and sheep of the Greek army at Troy. Those that escape the slaughter in the field, he leads back to his tent. Here he torments and slaughters them, thinking they are his intended prey, the Athenian generals Agamemnon, Menelaus, and Odysseus. It is at this point that we enter Sophocles' drama.

IN DEFENSE OF *ARETÉ*

Ajax, the earliest of Sophocles' surviving plays, opens with one of the truly remarkable scenes in all of Athenian tragedy. The time is just before dawn. The night is cold and visibility is poor. Odysseus is seen tracing Ajax's tracks in the sandy soil of the Trojan seashore near Ajax's tent. Then, at first unseen by him, the voice of Athena breaks the silence. Odysseus is startled, eventually recognizing the voice of his protector. There follows a remarkable scene in which a petulant and vindictive Athena plays condescendingly with Odysseus as if he were a child. She taunts him regarding his fear of seeing the "mad" Ajax. She had cruelly taunted Ajax, still in his delirium, making a fool of him in the midst of his slaughtered "captives."

Emerging from his divinely inspired madness, Ajax is shamed by his action. He decides that his dignity, his warrior and hero status — his *areté* — can only be restored if he commits suicide. His wife, Tekmessa, pleads with him to reconsider, as do his sailors from the fleet at Salamis, but to no avail. At this point one of the two supreme speeches in this play is delivered by Ajax: the speech to his very young son on what to expect from the vengeful Greeks, and how to live a life of honor. The other speech comes later, at the seashore, just before Ajax commits suicide using the sword given him as a gift by his most formidable enemy, the Trojan Hector.

Ajax's body is discovered by his wife and the Chorus of Sailors, and upon the entrance of Teukros, Ajax's brother, they set about to bury his body. They are prevented, first by Menelaus and then by Agamemnon, who hate Ajax. They order his body be thrown out to be devoured by animals. But Odysseus, no less an enemy of Ajax, intervenes. In the interest of reconciliation, he persuades his brother generals to permit the burial to go forward.

A PLAY DIVIDED?

It is the final third of the play that has been the victim of severe criticism. Many have said that the two parts of the play, the before and after of Ajax's suicide, are a polarity between Ajax and Odysseus. But nothing could be further from the truth. Neither of these two parts is an entity unto itself. The subject of both parts is quite simply a single one. John Moore has said, and rightly, that the death of Ajax "taken quite simply in itself, completes nothing; the play's action is complete only when the spectator is brought to an altered estimate of the meaning of Ajax's career and destiny." He continues:

> The major dramatic subject, the weight and heft of it, is Ajax.
> The greatness of his demand upon life is the thing that we
> must, above all, be made to feel; and Sophocles places this
> theme before us by the full dramatization he gives of Ajax'
> suffering and resolution, of the dismay and pathetic depend-
> ence of those around him, and of their desolation when his
> protection is removed.

REWRITING THE MYTH

Pindar, writing before Sophocles, chose to omit the insane slaughter of the livestock and the shame it brought, allowing Ajax's sole motivation for suicide to be the profound humiliation of not being awarded Achilles' armor — a slight of no minor dimension in the Homeric Age of Heroes. Sophocles, however, being a dramatist, saw far greater theatrical purchase in the more conventional version. Even as the sight of Ajax in his tent, surrounded by the gore of slaughtered beasts, presents a powerful theatrical image, it creates the enormously difficult dramaturgical problem of reestablishing Ajax as a great hero by the play's end. Concerning that scene of slaughter, says Moore, "it is a fearful and summary image of total degradation not merely of heroic, but of all human, value. The process by which this image is transformed and Ajax's disaster irradiated by his recovery of heroic strength and human relatedness is the true action of the play." By the end of the extended scene that begins with the slaughter in the tent, and continues with a speech to his young son Eurysakes, Ajax begins to reassert his noble and heroic self as he realizes the depravity of his action and understands that only the ultimate sacrifice will wipe his hero's slate clean. We are witness to a harsh and uncompromising ethic.

MAKING PEACE WITH LIFE AND DEATH

The second part of the reassertion of Ajax's honor comes at the seashore, where he sets up the scene for his suicide. The earlier bravado has tempered. He thinks about his loved ones: his son; his wife; whom he treated so cruelly in the previous scene, his mother and father home in Salamis — how each will react to his death. He asks the gods to allow him a quiet death, and that his brother Teukros find his body, sparing others the shock of the sight of it. All in all, he makes his peace with his life and his death. He does not seek peace with his surviving enemies, an act of reconciliation absent from Sophocles' scheme of things.

MATCHING FORM AND CONTENT

It is clear that the squabble among Teukros, Menelaus, and Agamemnon over the burial of Ajax's body is written in language less elegant than that which preceded it. Rather than see it as an artistic lapse, Sophocles is matching form with content. The speeches are unconscionably long, and the pettiness of the Greek leaders is an embarrassment, and meant to be precisely that. This was no doubt the Athenian audience's favorite part of the play. They thoroughly enjoyed debate with long speeches, a process fundamental to their politics. And to debate about burial was simply icing on the cake. For the modern audience, more conditioned to sound bites than diatribes, the image of the heroic Ajax gradually reemerging with great specificity and passion may well be the payoff of an evening with Ajax.

THE HERO AS SELF-MADE MAN

But what are we to make of the announcement of Athena, as related by the Greek seer Kalchas? She indicates that if Ajax is to survive, he must remain in his tent under the watch of his fellows for one whole day; otherwise his time is up. This is a shrewd move on Athena's part; she clearly knows Ajax totally. It is also consistent with the cruelty she displays toward Ajax in the play's prologue. As Cedric Whitman sees it, one day's disgrace for Ajax, at home, in his tent, under the watch of his men and Tekmessa — will mean that he "will have done the sensible thing — reason things out, yield honor lost, and reckon life worth more." But such a decision on Ajax's part — such "reasoning" — is an impossibility. If it were possible, he would no longer be Ajax, the man of action, the doer. For Athena to command him to stay in his tent for an entire day is simply to say that Ajax "cannot endure one day's disgrace." That is his *areté*, his honor, his greatness. That is why Ajax refuses Athena's help in battle to lead him to victory — an insane act of "superhuman pride and self-sufficiency," but self-sufficiency it is. But the hero, like no other mortal, has no choice but to be proud of his self-sufficiency, even as it leads him to destruction. A self-destruction in the search for personal glory is at the very core of the Greeks' understanding of the heroic temperament. If that is hubris, then so be it, and hubris must then be a "defense of *areté*." The hero is nothing more nor less than the self-made man, and he is accountable only to himself.

BEYOND LIFE

This behavior was "godlike" to Homer. It was the stuff of which Achilles was made, and the stuff of which Ajax, the greatest hero at Troy after Achilles, was also made. In them and in every true hero there is a *daemon*. This inner spirit, or spark, animates the being to an act or series of acts or life that is above the ordinary, a force we today might in more pejorative terms call daemonic. To quote Whitman again:

> The heroic assumption means precisely this — the possession of a standard which becomes a kind of fatal necessity that drives toward self-destruction. . . . It seems excessive and culpable only if one's standard is life and common sense; if one's standard is areté, it is an inevitable course. The true Greek hero raises the standard of his own excellence so high that he is no longer appropriate to life.

THE PASSING OF GREATNESS

Which leads us, in Sophocles' *Ajax*, to the wily, clever, ever devious and pragmatic Odysseus. If Ajax is the image of the uncompromising Homeric hero of centuries past, then Odysseus in this work is the paradigm of the ethic and temper of the time of Sophocles. He is a hero of compromise, not free of the use of deception, an attribute common to mid-fifth-century Athens. Athens was beginning the decline that would lead to her collapse with the conclusion of the Peloponnesian War in 404. If one were to think of a reason why Ajax and Odysseus should be enemies from a character standpoint, the vital question of compromise would serve splendidly. Ajax can never understand Odysseus and what motivates him. And so, we are left at the end of the play with a settlement that is tenuous at best. There is a vivid afterimage of a true hero of times past, and the direct image of a new hero in whom there is a mighty falling-off. The play's ending is deeply ironic as well as deeply felt by its author, and its closing moments lament the passing of greatness.

ANTIGONE

Since it is thought that *Antigone* was written in the middle of the fifth century, during Sophocles' vigorous middle years, it is not surprising that it fairly bursts with the youthful vitality and passion of Antigone and her fiancé, Haemon.

THE CONFLICT

The central conflict of the work revolves around the question: Who is right among two passionately held principles of Right? Creon, who puts all of his belief in the integrity of the State? Or Antigone, for whom political expediency is secondary, and who sides with compassion and piety to the dead in keeping with what she understands to be the eternal law of Justice? The specific issue arises over the burial of Antigone's brother Polynices, who unsuccessfully invaded Thebes. He was seeking to reclaim the throne that was usurped from him by his younger brother Eteocles. During the night prior to the opening of dramatic action, the brothers kill each other in battle. Creon, the new king of Thebes, issues an edict giving full rights of military burial to Eteocles, but denying them to Polynices. He also warns that anyone who buries Polynices will be stoned to death. Antigone refuses to honor the edict and carries out a ritual burial of her brother's corpse, which had been left to rot on the field of battle. She is apprehended and tries to justify her actions as a response to Creon's tyranny. Then she is walled up in a cavern to die, whereupon she takes her own life.

A LASTING DEBATE

The issue of whose action in this dramatic conflict is correct has been debated for millennia. Some say Creon, others Antigone. Still others see both equally right or equally wrong (evidently, moral equivalence goes back a long way). The stubbornness of both brings about the devastating tragedies suffered by each: Antigone dies, as does her devoted fiancé, Haemon; Creon suffers the loss of his son and his wife, and he longs for his own death.

Creon is shown as one who mouths principles of right government, all the right words: law and order. But then he roundly contradicts himself in action. He says that to govern well a king needs good advice but then lashes out at those who attempt to offer it to him. Creon talks the talk but doesn't walk the walk. Bowra, in his *Sophoclean Tragedy*, identifies Creon as the typical tyrant. Whitman sees him as nothing less, and in very historical terms:

> His quickness to wrath, his rejection of criticism, his suspicion of corruption among the people, his resentment of women, and his demand for utter servitude all find their parallels in the familiar habits of the great Greek tyrants.

A VOTE FOR ANTIGONE

Antigone was presented to an Athenian audience in the Theater of Dionysus at the height of the administration of Pericles, a ruler of goodness and brilliance whose rule is legendary in the history of Classical Athens. During this time, questions of Justice and Right and Statecraft were fiercely debated. No Athenian of the time would ever have tolerated a man who "behaved like a tyrant, and talked like an oligarch, however he sometimes prefaced his real sentiments with fine-sounding doctrines about the stability of the state," as Whitman writes. The government of the military state of Sparta was an example of such a state, whose stability was based on "repression, control from above, and suspicion." All of these were practiced by the Creon of *Antigone*. Again Whitman:

> It is therefore clear that Antigone's famous stubbornness, the fault for which she has been so roundly reproved, is really moral fortitude. She does not go "too far." How far should one go in resisting the tyranny of evil? Given real political areté, how much allegiance can one give to an illegal master? It is useless to speak of the defects of Antigone's qualities; there are no defects. Nor need there be any fault whereby her fall is justified. It is as foolish to try to justify it, as it would be to try to defend the legal murder of Socrates.

The idea that Creon shares a tragic fate with Antigone is grasping at straws. Indeed, he may fall and his world collapse around him, but there is nothing in him that is even remotely tragic. The tragedy belongs to those who are destroyed by his evil stupidity, and especially to Antigone, whose devotion to justice is unshakable. If modern history offers a solitary bravery in face of adversity to match hers, it is that of the student unflinchingly facing down the oncoming tanks in Tiananmen Square on the occasion of another, more recent demonstration of brutal tyranny.

THE WOMEN OF TRACHIS

In *The Women of Trachis* Sophocles sets himself much the same problem as he did in his earlier *Ajax*. One of his main characters, Deianira, dies two-thirds of the way through the play.

In *Ajax* the question is less who is the main character? But in *The Women of Trachis* it is precisely that: is the main character Deianira or Heracles? And Sophocles gives us precious little help when it comes to the title, which refers neither to Deianira nor to Heracles. Instead it refers to one of the least effective choruses in his extant body of work. This is a chorus that contributes virtually nothing to the dramatic action. The title, then, suggests that it is a deliberate evasion of the issue.

Many critics have also questioned whether Sophocles intended for Heracles, Deianira's husband, at his death by fire, to undergo elevation to divine status for his sufferings and join the pantheon of Olympian gods. It was a given in Greek mythology. But there is no mention of it in *The Women of Trachis*. And there is no implication that it is likely upon the play's conclusion, or even somewhere later in time. Does Sophocles expect the mythologically well-versed audience in the Theater of Dionysus to forget what it knows regarding the most famous hero of Greek mythology? If so, why?

HERACLES AS TRAGIC HERO?

Another problem, or surprise (depending on how one sees it), is the use of Heracles in a tragedy. He appears many times on the Classical Athenian stage. But he is primarily a comic figure, even a buffoon, and not infrequently in a drunken state. He is usually found in the comedy or the satyr play. In Euripides' *Alcestis* he appears as a comic figure despite the play's serious nature. But in *The Women of Trachis* he is seen as a fully serious character. He is a man who dies in excruciating pain because of a fatal but well-intentioned error on the part of his wife.

A NEW TAKE ON DEIANIRA

As for Deianira, she is without question one of Sophocles' — and Athenian tragedy's — most finely and sensitively etched portraits of a woman. She is kind, gentle, generous, keenly responsive to the feelings of others, and, above all, loving — even of a flagrantly philandering husband. His treatment of her is continuously boorish and insensitive. He is not only constantly absent but also a flagrant philanderer. In this play, he goes so far as to send his latest concubine home before his own arrival so that Deianira may tend to her needs.

If any leading female character in tragedy has an excuse to extinguish her husband for crudeness and cruelty it is Deianira. She is almost as highly motivated toward that end as Clytemnestra and more so even than Medea. And that is precisely what mythic tradition made of her prior to Sophocles: a strong, aggressive character — a kind of latter-day Amazon — whose name translates as nothing less than "husband killer." Though he kept the name, this is not the character that Sophocles chose to place at the center of his play *The Women of Trachis*.

TWO MINDS ON THE MATTER

From a purely dramaturgical standpoint, Deianira is the play's central, pivotal character. It is she who is the play's protagonist, she who is the doer, she who sets the tragedy in motion; without her there is no play. To be sure, what she does is in response to Heracles' inciting action, his absences and his affairs; but it is Deianira who reacts, observes, contemplates, decides, acts.

Sophocles could have omitted the physical appearance of Heracles entirely and reported his fate in one of his famous messenger speeches. In so doing he would have avoided the critical problem that has troubled critics and spectators. He might have chosen to avoid the Deianira character completely and focused his play entirely on the death of Heracles. In either case there would be no ongoing dispute about who is the central character of *The Women of Trachis*. But Sophocles chose neither course. Certain scholars have suggested that Sophocles was himself of two minds about who was the central character. I doubt this. What, then, may Sophocles have had in mind?

THE METAPHYSICS OF EVIL

Cedric Whitman has noted that with *The Women of Trachis* there enters into Sophocles' work a "gloomy change . . . an apparently sudden failure of the faith that gives the earlier works their reassuring brightness." And he places *The Women of Trachis* in the same category as the play that will follow it, *Oedipus the King*, as "another large step on [investigating] the metaphysics of evil, to which Sophocles devoted his life . . . "

Bitterness and destruction are the hallmarks of the plays of Sophocles' middle period, and they are "poisoned by a kind of universal despair," a despair that arises during the search for truth and knowledge. Whitman calls them plays of "tragic knowledge," knowledge that comes too late. In both *The Women of Trachis* and *Oedipus the King*, it is knowledge that brings with it not liberation and enlightenment but devastating loss.

For Sophocles. "humanity still wears its jewel of *areté*, but no apotheosis, like that of Antigone follows." Knowledge always does come, and the characters struggle to find it in time, but it always comes too late. The world to Sophocles in these plays is an irrational place in which his protagonists Deianira and Oedipus are "examples of high-minded humanity which wills the best and achieves the worst." Both of them suffer through no fault of their own; both are guiltless; and both lose everything: Deianira her life, and Oedipus all but his life; but that remaining scrap of life is overwhelmed by lost reputation, humiliation, and his depression. In The *Women of Trachis*, Sophocles' view of life had changed, or, rather, evolved. Whereas Antigone's death is likened to that of a goddess, for Deianira's death he provides no such comfort, not even in her own mind.

PRESENCE IN ABSENCE

The long final scene of *The Women of Trachis*, during which we witness Heracles' death agonies, includes a cruel but brilliantly conceived denial of redemption to Deianira. The vulgar and egocentric Heracles cares nothing about his wife's motivations. He refuses to listen to his son Hyllus's attempt to explain that Deianira had been afraid her husband was falling for the younger concubine Heracles had sent to her. As a result, she had used a love charm to make Heracles fall in love with her again. It had been given to her by a centaur, and she had no idea that the charm was poisoned.

It takes little stretch of imagination to see Deianira ever present onstage during the final third of the play. If her corpse were to be dumped onstage and remain in full view, she would not have greater presence. What we see is the result of her doing, and Heracles insanely refuses to see her side of it and the good intention behind her action. If he had, there would surely have been a reconciliation, an ending that Sophocles did not want to write. At the play's end, Sophocles is simply, and finally, emphasizing what has been his point all along: that the best of intentions may lead to a tragic outcome and do so in a most ignominious way. It is the final nail in Deianira's casket. She has lived alone and unloved and remains so in death.

ZEUS'S HANDIWORK

But the play is not just about Deianira, though she may dominate it by the length of her role and her goodness of character. It is also about Heracles, however late he enters. Early in the play, the chorus piously asserts that Zeus always cares for his children. The reference, of course, is to Heracles, who is literally a child of Zeus. But that piety does not materialize in regard either to Zeus' true son or to his metaphoric "daughter," the totally human Deianira.

But what of Sophocles' reason for omitting any mention of the traditional apotheosis of Heracles after his suffering and death by fire?

All we are given is the implacably cruel universe that Sophocles appears to be asserting, one in which human *areté* no longer counts for anything, as it once did in *Antigone*, and as it might still in the case of Heracles. For all his indifference to and final hatred of his wife, he spent his life and labors in the service of good. How could the author permit even a single exception to his pessimistic view of existence by allowing whatever good Heracles, the greatest of Greek heroes, may have done, to be rewarded in the traditional way? If we take Sophocles seriously, no such exception is possible. He had very good reason to alter tradition, even to hope that the audience could forget it, and put in its place the philosophical view of universal evil and malignancy that he intended to show as the rationale for the action of his tragedy. If not even Heracles, the spawn of Zeus, is spared, how could a mere mortal hope to be?

Hyllus's words that close the play are unequivocal: that all the horrors and evils that have transpired are the handiwork of Zeus.

OEDIPUS THE KING

Sophocles' *Oedipus the King* is perhaps, along with *Hamlet*, the Western World's best-known dramatic work. *Oedipus the King*, like every great play, is based on the simplest of premises, the premise of every murder mystery ever told: who is the murderer? It is as simple as that. It is a whodunit. Every action in the play comes from the search for the murderer. In theatrical jargon it is the "through-line." *Hamlet*, for all of its complexity, is every bit as simple at its root. The sentinel Bernardo, who utters the play's first line, states it as baldly as possible: "Who's there?" There is the through-line. From there on, the dramatic search at its most basic level is to discover the validity of the Ghost of Hamlet's father. Faced with the Ghost, Hamlet asks: "Be thou a spirit of health or goblin damned, / Bring with thee airs from heaven or blasts from hell . . ." Everything hinges on the answer. If from heaven, the Ghost can be trusted and Hamlet can act accordingly, taking revenge on his uncle Claudius for the murder of his father. If from hell, the Ghost is demonic and out to compromise Hamlet's soul. In each great play, the central and most basic question is immediately made clear.

In *Oedipus the King* it is crystal clear from the very moment that Creon enters, with a message from Apollo, that the question is who is the murderer of King Laios? This does not mean that higher, more philosophical issues are not also being sought out and tested. Many issues are explored, such as Oedipus's parentage, his very identity, his courage in the face of extreme adversity, his self-indictment for the murder of his father and marriage to his mother. Truth is required of Oedipus at every turn of fate. A question always facing the spectator of Oedipus's dilemma is will he or will he not serve as his own judge, jury, and executioner?

FATHER OF HIS PEOPLE

With each succeeding scene of the play, Oedipus is faced with new information that further implicates him in the crime that Apollo says must be punished and expiated before Thebes can be purged of the plague. At each scene's end, Oedipus, pushed to the extreme, retreats into the palace in a highly agitated state. He returns after the Chorus's thoughtful meditation on the preceding scene. He is calm again and determined to push on into deeper waters. This is not to imply that he does so without fear; if so, where would be the dramatic tension that will mount to a shattering climax?

One way of looking at the play's structure is in terms of opposites — what a musician would call counterpoint: one note pitted against another, upward and downward musical motion simultaneously enacted. This defines precisely the progress of *Oedipus the King*. For every notch on the material scale that Oedipus falls, he rises a notch on the moral scale. If when he speaks of himself in the play's first speech as "I, Oedipus, known to everyone," it has nothing to do with the old

cliché hammered away at in too many classrooms, that Oedipus suffers
from "overweening" pride, that he is haughty, that he is remote, that
he is more interested in himself than he is in his people and his city.
And yet these truisms are on many a student's and teacher's tongue and
prove very difficult to shake free and deposit into the universal recycle
bin of misconceived information.

MAN OF ACTION

Oedipus is not extravagant in his self-praise (if indeed that is what it
is). He once saved Thebes from the clutches of the Sphinx and single-
handedly restored it to health. He did what no one, not even Apollo's
prophet in Thebes, Tiresias, was able to accomplish. And for that he
has won the reputation with the people of Thebes of being their savior
when all else failed. Oedipus is aware of this. How could he not be?
And in the nineteen or so years since that event, he has proven himself
time and again as a "people's" king. His eye is always on the welfare of
his "children," as he calls his subjects in his opening lines.

So aware is Oedipus of his mission in regard to Thebes and its
people that he has spent sleepless nights in a state of profound anxiety,
weeping for his people's pain, his thoughts groping in every direction
for a cure until finally he found one and set immediately to work. He
acted — and action is at the very core of Oedipus's being. He sent
Creon to Delphi to learn from Apollo the cause of the plague and the
remedy for it. Enough cannot be said about the place of action in Oedipus's method of operating. It is so much a part of his nature that virtually his every speech is in the active voice. If Oedipus speaks of himself
in his opening lines as "known to everyone," it is not ego, not false
pride, not hubris that is being displayed. But it is a healthy knowledge
of himself and of the position that he holds in the estimation of his
people for deeds of enlightened good undertaken for their well-being.

According to Nick Fisher, in his *Oxford Classical Dictionary* article
on *hubris,* to conceive of hubris as "pride, over-confidence, or any

behavior which may offend divine powers, rests, it is now generally held, on misunderstanding of ancient texts, and concomitant and over-simplified views of Greek attitudes to the gods have lent support to many doubtful, and over-Christianizing, interpretations, above all of Greek tragedy." In Aristotle's definition of *hubris* he states quite clearly that hubris gives pleasure, and "the cause of the pleasure for those committing hubris is that by harming people, they think themselves superior . . ." To see the compassionate and people-directed Oedipus of the play's opening as hubristic is, therefore, seriously to misread and misinterpret the motives of a man who is justly honored as a man, not as a god, by his grateful people. The old Priest of Apollo says quite clearly to Oedipus at the start that he and the people of Thebes "haven't come because we think of you as of a god; no, we know you to be a man and only a man; all of us know this, even the young, crouching here." Sophocles could not have been more explicit in his definition through action of the nature of his hero's profound humanity. According to Fisher: "Hubris is most often the insulting infliction of physical force or violence," a far cry from anything in the history of Oedipus, including his killing of Laius, a situation, as Oedipus explains in *Oedipus at Colonus*, that offered the prospect of kill or be killed.

Finally, in hope of hammering the ultimate nail in the coffin of this issue, we turn again to Fisher:

> Nor is it helpful to see Greek tragedy centrally concerned to display the divine punishment of hubristic heroes; tragedy focuses rather on unjust or problematic suffering, whereas full-scale acts of hubris by the powerful tend to deprive them of the human sympathy necessary for tragic victims.

How easy it would be for Oedipus, unwittingly self-condemned as he is, to put an end to the search for the murderer of Laius, and thus save himself the agony of self-incrimination and the punishment contingent upon it. Had he done so, he would indeed have been guilty of hubris for his "infliction of physical force or violence" on the plague-infested, suffering, and innocent people of Thebes by not liberating his city from it. But that is not what happens. With every reappearance of Oedipus on the scene after a major setback of new, self-implicating information, he rises to greater and greater moral stature for not shirking his duty — to discover the truth for the good of his people: who is the murderer of Laius? Given the contrary-motion structure of this play, when Oedipus reaches the lowest point of his physical existence, blind, self-exiled, utterly destitute, and in a state of abject misery, he at the same time reaches the epitome of implicit moral transcendence though he may himself not realize it. He has punished himself in the most merciless way possible for the two-pronged crime of killing his father and marrying his mother. So careful a moralist is Oedipus when dealing with his unwitting moral infraction that rather than escape his condition through death, he chooses, freely, to expiate crimes that he committed without knowing. If knowledge comes too late in Sophocles' tragic scheme of things, it comes to Oedipus in this play in a way so devastating that he has throughout the millennia become the tragic moral hero par excellence.

FATE HAS NOTHING TO DO WITH IT

There is one further issue, which is perhaps the most important, that demands comment regarding Classical Athenian tragedy, and, in particular, *Oedipus the King*. That is the question of Fate. *Oedipus the King* is widely, and mistakenly, known as "the tragedy of fate." This is a tragedy in itself, for it unwittingly consigns one of the supreme achievements of the human mind to the trash heap of inevitability.

Perhaps more than any other, Freud's statement in his seminal work of 1900, *The Interpretation of Dreams*, supplied fuel for this interpretation. He writes: "The *Oedipus Rex* is a tragedy of fate: its tragic effect depends on the conflict between the all-powerful will of the gods and the vain efforts of human beings threatened with disaster; resignation to the divine will, and the perception of one's own impotence is the lesson which the deeply moved spectator is supposed to learn from the tragedy." He concludes the passage by saying: "It may be that we were all destined to direct our first sexual impulses towards our mothers, and our first impulses of hatred towards our fathers; our dreams convince us that we were."

It is difficult to belittle one of the most provocative and contested intellectual concepts of the modern world, the "Oedipus complex," whatever one may think of it. But it is wrong to accept Freud's observation regarding the critical problem of fate in Sophocles' play. This is especially important when one remembers that Freud himself made a distinction between the Sophoclean work and the myth on which it was based. Later in *The Interpretation of Dreams* he writes: "The form which it [the Oedipus myth] subsequently assumed [namely the *Oedipus Tyrannus*] was the result of an uncomprehending secondary elaboration of the material, which sought to make it serve a theological intention."

This issue of fate plays a large part in a major study of Sophocles' play by Bernard Knox, *Oedipus at Thebes*, and he expresses the problem as succinctly and brilliantly as possible when he writes:

No amount of symbolic richness — conscious, subconscious, or unconscious — will create dramatic excitement in a play which does not possess the essential prerequisites of human free will and responsibility. The tragedy must be self-sufficient: that is, the catastrophe must be the result of the free decision and action (or inaction) of the tragic protagonist . . . If the *Oedipus Tyrannus* is a "tragedy of fate," the hero's will is not free, and the dramatic efficiency of the play is limited by that fact. The problem is insoluble; but luckily the problem does not exist to start with. For in the play which Sophocles wrote the hero's will is absolutely free and he is fully responsible for the catastrophe. Sophocles has very carefully arranged the material of the myth in such a way as to exclude the external factor in the life of Oedipus from the action of the tragedy. The action is not Oedipus' fulfillment of the prophecy, but his discovery that he has already fulfilled it. The catastrophe of Oedipus is that he discovers his own identity; and for this discovery he is first and last responsible. The main events of the play are in fact not even part of the prophecy: Apollo predicted neither the discovery of the truth, the suicide of Jocasta, nor the self-blinding of Oedipus. In the actions of Oedipus in the play "fate" plays no part at all.

ELECTRA

Electra is like no other play by Sophocles. It is an in-depth character study during the first half of which nothing Electra does serves to further the plot. What it does do, however, is make unforgettably clear the agony her life has been since the murder of her father, Agamemnon, by her mother, Clytemnestra.

A QUESTION OF MORALITY

Perhaps the most troublesome question that the play raises is its morality. It was written more than forty years after Aeschylus's *The Libation Bearers*, in which Orestes murders his mother. In Sophocles' play, Orestes does not show signs of conscience or remorse. This is not true in Aeschylus's play. In Aeschylus, Orestes is riddled by conscience for killing his mother. He is pursued by the avenging Furies at that play's end and in the succeeding drama, *The Eumenides*. Though the Furies are mentioned in Sophocles' play, they do not materialize after the murder as forces of retribution for the murder of a mother by her son. Is morality being held in abeyance in Sophocles' play by design, in order to emphasize its unrelenting viciousness? For example, Sophocles has Orestes ask Apollo's oracle at Delphi not whether he should kill his mother, but how? In any event, at the play's end Orestes has done his filial duty and emerges triumphant and unconflicted, like the radiant star of fortune to which he compares himself in the prologue.

RICH IN THEATRICAL MOMENTS

The play has many startlingly theatrical moments. The scene of Clytemnestra's offstage murder by Orestes is one of the highpoints of Athenian tragedy for the cruelty and viciousness of its execution. Consider the image of Electra pacing the stage like a caged animal, then suddenly let loose and running up to the great doors of the palace and screaming to get on with the murder. Her screams start again once the first strike has been delivered. These are masterstrokes of stagecraft. And the so-called recognition scene, when Electra discovers that it is really Orestes who is present and that he is not dead, is one of the transcendent moments in World Theater. So high is the intensity of this moment that there is no alternative but for Electra and Orestes to burst into song. No mere words, however exalted, could have expressed their rapture.

A different sort of theatrical moment is the heart-wrenching scene in which Electra carries the urn in which she believes her beloved brother's ashes are contained almost as though she is nursing it. She addresses it and refuses to allow it to be taken from her arms by her still-unrecognized brother. There is also the excitement of the Tutor's narration of the chariot-race accident at Delphi in which Orestes is said to have been killed. The strength of this scene resides not so much in the narration (which we know is a fiction), but in the effect that the fiction has on Electra. At the end of it, her grasp on life is tenuous at best. Her hope and expectation for just revenge have been demolished. And yet, so strong is Electra's character, which is to say her passion and her determination to survive, that she adds a new dimension to Sophocles' art.

HEROIC ENDURANCE

Sophocles has shown in previous plays that the human being is in possession of a divine spark (daemon/*areté*) that is nothing less than the will to see justice done. *Electra* is an outstanding example of that belief. Quite simply, *Electra* is *Antigone* revisited (the plays' structures are remarkably similar). Electra is no less headstrong than Antigone, no less unrelenting, nor any less determined to see justice done. She has simply suffered more intensely, and for an unspeakably longer time. Consequently she has become possessed by her mission to the point that she is close to madness. And that difference between her and Antigone is what separates them, for all their closeness, and puts the play into the final phase of Sophocles' development. This is a period that Whitman calls Tragic Endurance. Sophocles' last three extant plays are in this period: *Electra*, *Philoctetes*, and *Oedipus at Colonus*. Whitman continues:

> Sophocles' last period is 'purgatorial,' in that it deals with the soul's use of time. The emphasis, however, is not on the purging of sin, for the characters are not sinful; the emphasis is on heroic endurance in the loneliness of heroic rightness . . . . In the *Ajax* and *Antigone* areté triumphed by a kind of phoenix death: out of the fiery ordeal arose an indestructible historic vision. In *The Trachiniae* and *Oedipus Rex*, although human virtue fulfilled its function without failure, life itself seemed an indignity no virtue could surmount. The three last works are very mysterious for all their brightness of atmosphere. Man's best has again begun to count. His inward divinity brings him closer to the gods themselves, or — since that phrase is perhaps meaningless — to a larger transcendent idea of the divine and eternal, which ratifies and seals the striving divinity of the human, or at least of the heroic sphere.

If that inward divinity of Ajax and Antigone arises out of their extinction, another major difference between them and Electra is that she does not have to die in order to have her "spirit" rise from her "ashes." In Sophocles' plays, death was once a necessity. It was part of the Homeric hero/warrior ethic. Now it is metaphoric. In these last three plays, death is no longer a requirement for the humanistic transformation of the hero. There is a flame or a spirit that rises out of the ashes of Ajax and Antigone. In Electra, the spirit is rekindled between the conclusion of the death-narration and early in the following scene with Chrysothemis.

It is in that scene that Electra announces that she will accomplish the mission on her own, with or without her sister's help. She has no verbal transition, but only an internal transition. In many respects this sequence is alchemical in its structure. In the death-narration, Electra is plunged into the lowest, blackest depths. Out of this "death" state there begins to emerge the spark of renewal that Whitman calls the "inward divinity . . . which ratifies and seals the striving divinity of the human . . . sphere." Structurally speaking, from that moment on everything assumes an upward curve, as opposed to the downward spiral of everything regarding Electra that went before. No longer must the hero be physically destroyed in order to rise spiritually in triumph. It is now Sophocles' view that the hero must survive physically, but be destroyed spiritually. And out of that spiritual destruction the hero can rise triumphant. But one factor of this new equation is still missing, and that is Time.

TIME

Oedipus the King precedes *Electra*. At the moment when Oedipus is in possession of all but the last bit of the truth he needs to convict himself, he experiences a transcendental insight in which he declares himself the "child of Chance." Chance is his mother, he announces. And his brothers are the passing months that have seen him "great and small in Time." That moment of illumination passes as rapidly as it arrives. It is not to be heard of again until *Electra*, where it becomes a key function in Sophocles' view of existence. For Time allows for suffering, suffering for endurance, and endurance together with suffering for enlightenment, transformation, and transcendence. Although Electra may not be the supreme manifestation of that progress, she is a first step as far as the last three extant plays of Sophocles are concerned.

TAKING THE STAGE

In Aeschylus's and Euripides' versions of the story it is the murder of Clytemnestra by Orestes that is the climax. In Sophocles' *Electra*, the climax is Electra's victory and her release from decades of inhuman treatment by her mother and Aegisthus. The suffering she has undergone over a long period of time would have destroyed all but the strongest individual. But Electra perseveres against all odds. The first half of the play demonstrates that. When the greatest of those odds strikes her in the form of the "death" of Orestes, on whom all her hope is founded, she restructures her mental and physical universe. Without hesitation she assumes the burden of accomplishing the deed herself.

By the time Orestes finally becomes known to her, his function in the operation has become virtually superfluous. Batya Laks has written a brilliant study of some of the *Electra* plays from Aeschylus to the present. He suggests with considerable ingenuity that the appearance of Orestes may be seen as the visualization of Electra's resolve to fulfill her mission of justified vengeance herself — Peter Brook's notion of making the invisible visible. So, if Sophocles' play does not deal with the moral question of Orestes' killing of his mother, it is because that was not Sophocles' intention. It must be noted, as well, that from as far back as Homer and on up to Aeschylus's *The Libation Bearers*, Orestes is portrayed, in Whitman's words, as "a stainless hero, whose act was looked upon as the deliverance of his country."

Many have seen Orestes as the play's central figure. If there is any lingering doubt that it is Electra who is the play's central figure, Sophocles settles it with a brilliant theatrical gesture that needs no words: Orestes and Pylades herd Aegisthus off into the palace to kill him. This leaves Electra, of all the main characters of the play, onstage, alone. As James Hogan has said: "Clearly, the revenge of Orestes is but the context for this play, not its dominant thematic or dramatic point."

PHILOCTETES

Produced at the City Dionysia in Athens in 409, *Philoctetes* is the next to the last play written by the aged Sophocles, and the last he was to see in production. It is also one of the two plays by him that can be dated with any certainty. The other is *Oedipus at Colonus*, produced in 401, five years after his death.

ENTER NATURE

These final two plays share certain attributes that distinguish them from Sophocles' other extant plays. First of all, they take place in remote regions. There is about their setting and ambiance something both mysterious and sacred. The grove of the Eumenides in *Oedipus at Colonus* is described almost at once to the blind old beggar Oedipus by his daughter Antigone as being exceedingly tranquil. Laurel, olive, and vines abound, with only the songs and rushing of wings of nightingales disturbing the silence. It is a sacred place. In *Philoctetes* the area is even more remote. It is the island of Lemnos, which is uninhabited and desolate, with nothing but the sound of waves languidly lapping the shore, the soaring of birds, winds rushing, rain, hot, and cold. Every page is infused with these images.

Nature has arrived in these two final plays of the old playwright, and in such profusion that it threatens to overwhelm the works themselves with its power. Considering the subject matter — time, suffering, endurance, and resolution — Nature is perhaps the only suitable setting. This is true first because there is nothing more basic. And second, because, as in the most profound and the brightest of Shakespeare's comedies, the resolution of conflict is achieved in Nature's Forest of Arden without tragic loss or destruction of property or life.

MORAL DOUBLE BIND

In *Philoctetes* Sophocles introduces a new kind of character to the
Athenian stage. In *Electra* Sophocles presents a profound in-depth
character study, but one that is one-dimensional. In Neoptolemus, the
young son of the great Achilles, who is now dead, we have a new kind
of hero whose dilemma is unique in Athenian tragedy. He is a man in a
double bind. He is caught between allegiance to his senior officers at
Troy, the Atreidai, and allegiance to his conscience. His mission is to
return the abandoned, snakebite-wounded Philoctetes to Troy. Then
together, as the oracle tells it, they may assault the walls of Troy and
win the already-ten-year-long campaign. Odysseus, Neoptolemus's
superior officer, orders him to bring Philoctetes back by trickery and
deception, because persuasion will not work. But deception is not in
Neoptolemus's nature, any more than it was part of his noble father's
nature. Neoptolemus would rather bring Philoctetes back by force
than by deceit. This is especially true because Philoctetes is incapaci-
tated by his wound and not likely to get the better of them. In
Watling's words the conflict is between

> physical weakness plus moral strength versus physical
> superiority plus moral weakness. Philoktêtês is physically at
> the mercy of his opponents, Neoptolemos and Odysseus,
> who could easily force their will upon him, and almost do so;
> but, as Neoptolemos well knows, might is not right, and
> without right (here symbolized by the bow in the hands of
> its rightful owner) might cannot prosper.

GETTING PRIORITIES RIGHT

Neoptolemus at the start of the play is not entirely against the under-
handed proposition of the wily and unscrupulous Odysseus, though he
objects to deceitful actions. He does, after all, capitulate too readily
when Odysseus promises him two prizes if he carries through the

maneuver. Odysseus offers him the reputation for courage and intelligence. "All right, I'll so it, and farewell shame," says the young man. As Odysseus said earlier, he could be virtuous some other day. A reputation for courage and intelligence are too powerful to pass by. But honor and nobility of mind are not so easily overcome in this young noble son of Achilles. He discovers this in the process of carrying through his deceptive maneuvers. In the end, after mighty moral struggles and internal conflict, he places his allegiance on the side of the wronged hero Philoctetes. As Watling sees it: "The sympathetic and sensitive picture of Neoptolemus gives the play an unusual charm and is one of Sophocles' highest achievements in character-drawing."

But the central character of Sophocles' play is not the fascinating Neoptolemus, it is the tragically derailed hero Philoctetes. Ten years before, on the way to Troy, he stopped off at the island of Chryse to offer prayers and sacrifices to the local deity for success in the campaign. It is there that he is bitten seemingly without motivation in the foot by the guardian snake of the goddess. The wound fails to heal, it suppurates, it becomes unbearable. The wounded man's cries disturb the entire camp, and his malady refuses to heal. As a result, Odysseus abandons him on the desolate and uninhabited island of Lemnos. It is here Philoctetes remains for ten years untended, in misery, and in mortifying pain. It is only now, a decade later, that an oracle advises that Troy will be taken only by Philoctetes and Neoptolemus, using Philoctetes' magically endowed bow, a gift from Heracles. Arrows from this bow never miss their mark.

But for all of the interest in Neoptolemus, it is still Philoctetes who is the central character on whom time, suffering, and endurance do their work. It is at first glance difficult to say whether this trinity of Sophoclean values weighs greater on Philoctetes or on Electra. It is close. Both of them are outcasts, with Philoctetes the greater put upon as he is also the bearer of an insufferably painful foot that he must drag from one end of the island to the other in search of sustenance. He has had no choice but to carry out this miserable task for ten years. From a societal standpoint Electra's situation is also better. She has her group of women to support her, whereas Philoctetes has no one; he is completely isolated and, unlike Electra, for no discernible fault of his own. Her "fault" is a relentless pursuit of justice that alienates her from all but a few.

HEROISM TESTED

What now emerges as a central issue in *Philoctetes* concerns the moral dilemma that arises when the well-being of an individual is in conflict with that of society. Society, having rejected Philoctetes in as extreme a way as possible by abandoning him on an uninhabited island, now wants to reclaim him, needing him in order to win the Trojan War. But Philoctetes, the victim of society's cruelty, now, ten years later, rejects the same society that made him an outcast. Whitman adds to this equation: "but the beggar now rejects society and is brought back into it only by his own resistance to it." And he continues:

> The problem is just such a paradox as Sophocles loved and could manipulate with consummate skill; one may see at a glance that his discovery of truth in the utterly paradoxical — the unexpected and unexpectable — is an extension of his concern with the lateness of knowledge. But he is concerned now with a further ridge of knowledge, the knowledge of those who are already plunged in misery [unlike Aias and Dêianeira] and yet endure. For them [Philoktêtês and Oedipus at Kolonos] the paradox is benign, time fights for their dignity, and the knowledge they gain is the knowledge of a victory implicit in a standard higher, or at least more remote, than the norm.

And by "norm" Whitman means the merely human, with no negative reflection from the term *merely*. If the merely human were enough for the heroic nature, then, as Segal rightly puts it, the play would logically have ended with line 1408 in the Greek text. This is where Neoptolemus tells Philoctetes to say his farewell to Lemnos and kiss the ground: "Both men are confirmed in the heroism of their essential natures: Neoptolemus, in his courage, compassion, and sense of honor; Philoctetes, in his ability to endure suffering, his strength of will, and his moral integrity. But the oracles have made it clear that heroism serves a larger purpose" — that larger purpose being service to the societal collective as opposed to the merely personal, which at this point in the play requires that both men turn their backs on society and serve their own ends.

Sophocles had been working with this idea in mind, albeit in embryo. In one of his earliest extant plays, *Antigone*, the defender of societal (and divine) justice is destroyed. In *Philoctetes*, for the first time, he creates a situation in which a far vaster point of reference is introduced. In this play he allows the hero to rise above his personal integrity, even against his own will and sense of justice, and to survive on a level of heroic endeavor that surpasses all else. To accomplish this, Sophocles introduces one of the rare appearances of a deus ex machina, the god from the machine, in his extant work. But it is not the god that Euripides might have used who emerges at the end to unravel a plot that has become too complex for the mere mortal mind to deal with. The Heracles who appears in the last few pages of *Philoctetes* is an organic plot device that serves many sublime as well as merely human purposes.

To Cedric Whitman, the appearance of Heracles at the play's end is the visualization of Philoctetes' heroic divinity, his daemon, his *areté*:

> And suddenly his victory appears to him. There are few
> moments in drama more breath-taking than this one.
> Heracles is divine, but his divinity comes from within
> Philoctetes. He explains this at once by comparing his own
> hard toils, and the 'immortal areté' which rewarded them,
> with Philoctetes' sufferings and his glory to come. Heracles is
> Philoctetes' own special god who gave him his bow when he

ascended to heaven. . . . He is the archetype of Philoctetes' greater self, the pattern of his glory. And what is this "immortal areté"? If it is immortal, it is because it is a god in man, the yardstick by which he measures himself against fate and circumstance. And even the gods themselves. The whole burden of Heracles' revelation is areté. The words keep flashing out. . . .

To which Charles Segal adds that Heracles

also represents a more objective, less individually centered order, and from that too Philoctetes has long been estranged. Restored to that order, he will now find his proper, decisive rôle. His endurance on Lemnos has constituted a test of heroism as arduous as the sufferings of the Greeks on the battlefield of Troy. But heroism is not fulfilled in a vacuum [which is to say in a non-societal venue]; it requires a context, both human and divine.

A WORLD OF IMPERFECT JUSTICE

It is important to note that what Heracles tells Philoctetes is nothing new to him. He has already heard it all from Neoptolemus. "But now," says Whitman, "Philoctetes himself has resolved on these things, and the resolution is like a god awakening in him. It is a vision of sudden spiritual liberation which can scarcely be paralleled elsewhere." Prior to this "liberation," Philoctetes had rejected his divinely determined destiny, delivered to him by the oracle, and thereby had rejected the gods themselves. The gods ordained that he could only be healed if he helped his personal enemies, the generals, Odysseus, and the Athenian army, to overcome Troy. Yet the acceptance of the will of the gods is, as Segal says, "to become free of the disease." To effect this outcome is the reason for Heracles' appearance. It is why Heracles directs Philoctetes to exhibit piety toward the gods. He does so, enabling the final realignment to be realized. Philoctetes, by accepting, is reintegrated into both society and the order of the gods. He now sees his destiny in the largest terms possible rather than the merely personal. For that is the function of the Sophoclean hero.

Philoctetes reenters the world with a test of himself still to be realized. It is perhaps the most important and difficult test of all: "to accept life and action in a world of imperfect justice." But now, given Philoctetes' transformation, gained through years of suffering and endurance, it is certain that his hard-won integrity will never again be vulnerable to the Odysseuses of the world. "The play moves," says Segal, "toward reconciliation at the end, but Sophocles does not obscure the gap that still remains between men and gods and between base men and the noble heroes whom they have victimized." That gap will be filled in Sophocles' final play when the blind beggar Oedipus is welcomed into the company of the gods.

OEDIPUS AT COLONUS

The aged Sophocles chose the characters that had brought him his greatest success as his farewell to the theater and to life. *Oedipus at Colonus* is a play that has been called apocalyptic. And so it is, if for no other reason than that the gods who have been so elusive in the plays of Sophocles, so distant and so irrationally evil, finally are humbled by the tragic endurance of a man who refuses to give up against all the odds that the gods and he himself have stacked against him.

ON THE ROAD

For all its length, *Oedipus at Colonus* is an extremely simple play structurally. The old Oedipus has wandered aimlessly for many years in exile from Thebes. Blinded, he arrives at the sacred grove at Colonus. His clothes are torn and ragged, his hair straggling, and his skin so encrusted with dirt that dirt and skin are indistinguishable from one another. His companion these many years, his daughter Antigone, has endured a life not unlike her father's.

THE ACCEPTANCE OF LIFE'S ADVERSITIES

Oedipus at Colonus has been criticized as static and lacking action, and to a superficial observer this may indeed be the case. But action in Sophoclean tragedy may atypically be defined as "the functioning of the hero's will, in whatever form," as Whitman has it. And Oedipus's will here is in constant and powerful function from the moment he learns that he has arrived at the place predicted for him by Apollo years ago: Colonus. He vows never to leave. During his years of wandering and depravation, Oedipus has risen to a near-divine level of wisdom and spiritual enlightenment. This is a transcendence that has transpired in time. Time plays a major role in this play, for time alone offers the possibility of suffering. And in Sophocles' work, suffering is the great purger of material concerns. "Suffering and time," says Oedipus shortly after his arrival at Colonus, "vast time, have taught me acceptance of life's adversities, as has nobility of birth."

It may have taught him acceptance, perhaps, but not forgiveness, not humility. Herein lies the source of energy that drives this final play of Sophocles to its transcendent conclusion. Time may have done its work on Oedipus, but it has not softened a nature that (to use a phrase that is uncannily apt) has been "more sinned against than sinning." Time, distance, and the razor-sharp edge of objectivity have demonstrated to Oedipus that, though he once punished himself mercilessly for the unspeakable sins of killing his father and marrying his mother, he was not in any way guilty of those crimes. In some of the play's most powerful lines, Oedipus defends himself against even his former self. He killed in self-defense, he rightly affirms, when his life was threatened. He had no way of knowing the nature of the marriage he entered into at the insistence of the people of Thebes when they offered him power and the throne for his liberation of them and their city from the Sphinx. He castigates at length the aged Creon, who comes to claim him as a talisman to protect Thebes against future aggression by Athens. And Oedipus disowns his sons, one of whom, Polynices, has come to seek his support of a seven-pronged assault on Thebes to regain the throne from his usurping brother, Eteocles. When he needed their help, accuses the raging Oedipus, they turned their backs on him, and he curses them to suffer the consequence of mutual brother-murder.

If these tirades of the ancient Oedipus were couched purely in animosity engendered in the past, they just might be excessive. They are, on the other hand, enlivened and made volatile in the present by virtue of issues that bear immediately upon the present and that only indirectly look back to the past. Creon appears on the scene after the most recent oracle from Delphi informs him that Oedipus's dead body will serve Thebes as protection against future attack. Creon insists on Oedipus's return, but he will not allow him to enter the city. Oedipus must reside outside its gates, as will his eventual grave. To add insult to injury, Creon arrives with military assistance sufficient to enforce his will. He proceeds to kidnap one of the daughters to force the issue, and threatens to take Oedipus prisoner if need be.

THE ARRIVAL OF POLYNICES AND DRAMATIC CONSTRUCTION

Polynices' arrival on the scene is prompted by his need to have Oedipus's support of his assault upon his brother, Eteocles. With Oedipus's support, the attack will succeed and Polynices and his troops will win; without the support of Oedipus, the campaign will fail. This situation dredges up the past for Oedipus, reminding him that his sons failed to defend him when they had the chance. The terrible addition of the present to this situation of long standing is Oedipus's virulent curse by which he not only disowns them but also damns them to slay each other in battle at Thebes.

Sophocles was a dramatist par excellence. He knew that to dredge up the past is not alone the basis for high drama. He understood that a new action must transpire immediately in full view of the spectator. He had learned that in *Oedipus the King*. His success in that regard in *Oedipus the King* made it one of the benchmarks of Western dramatic construction. Although *Oedipus at Colonus* may not be as swiftly moving as the earlier play, it is made of the same fabric.

THE END OF THE ROAD

Oedipus at Colonus is without question an old man's play, but in no way is it a tired play. Like Ibsen's *When We Dead Awaken*, it is a summation of everything that Sophocles' ninety-plus years have taught him. More important, however, it adds to his achievement in a way that would be startling at any age, let alone at his.

For the decades of his wandering, the blind Oedipus took whatever was offered, took whatever begging brought him. At his end he no longer takes. He gives; and what he gives is himself. In *Oedipus the King*, he declares himself to be the brother of the passing months that have seen him small and great in time. In this final play, in his final hours, he arrives at a status that transcends time. It has been a long road, a long haul to an end that reaches out beyond mortal concerns. The fact that Oedipus knows in life that his dead body will be a gift beyond compare (he announces it in the opening moments) tells us without any contradiction that he has already transcended time. He is a hero, and he knows it. This is all the more remarkable, for traditionally, heroic stature is achieved only in death. Oedipus has, quite simply, already arrived. He has achieved cult status. His road, his tragic endurance, have burned away his fallibility, and he sees for the first time with eyes freed of mortality. Everything that the earlier Oedipus plays set out is here systematically put into laborious and slow-grinding reverse.

No sooner has the despairing and rejected Polynices departed than the final movement of the play falls into gear. The gods who played so loosely and cruelly with the old man acknowledge him with the rumble of their divine thunder and the flash of Zeus's lightning. These are sure signs that they are present and their announcement that the end is at hand and that the process of transformation/ transfiguration is begun. All at once the bent, groping, and shuffling Oedipus stands erect. Where once he was led, he now leads. Where once he sought help, he now gives it. A long-arriving inner vision has asserted itself: he is complete, and he looks out from within Time. The gods even call to him, urging him on and unleashing panic in those assembled: "Oedipus! Oedipus! It's time! You stay too long!"

HOLY ATHENS

In this final work, Sophocles not only brings his life's work to an incomparable conclusion, he also lays a blessing on the deme, or district, that gave him birth, Colonus. He also blesses Athens, the city that nurtured not only him, but, more important, a society and a government and a cultural achievement that the world has scarcely approximated since. Ajax's sailors, in the play that bears his name, sing of Athens in terms that can only have come from the full heart of one of its greatest sons:

> What joy is left me now,
>> what joy? O if only my sails
>>> were set for home! Set
>> for Sounion's tree-topped summit
>>> that rears above the sea-washed rocks,
>>>> and greet, sailing into sight,
>>> the blessèd city,
>>>> my holy Athens!

The tragedy is that by the time of the posthumous production of *Oedipus at Colonus* in 401, Athens had fallen to Sparta in the Peloponnesian War. This war tore Greece apart between 431 and 404. It was a fate that Sophocles cannot have failed to foresee as he wrote *Oedipus at Colonus* in 406, and that must have caused him great pain and sadness.

DRAMATIC MOMENTS

from the Major Plays

These short excerpts are from the playwright's major plays. They give a taste of the work of the playwright. Each has a short introduction in brackets that helps the reader understand the context of the excerpt. The excerpts, which are in chronological order, illustrate the main themes mentioned in the In an Hour essay. Premiere date is given.

CHARACTERS

> Athena (Athêna)
> Odysseus
> Ajax (Aias)

[This play traces the fate of the Greek warrior Ajax, following the events of the Iliad and the end of the Trojan War. Ajax is enraged that Odysseus, not he, was awarded the dead Achilles' armor. Due to a spell cast over him by Athena, he kills the cows and sheep, thinking that they are Greek warriors, his compatriots.]

ATHÊNA: Odysseus, son of Laërtês!
　　I always seem to find you in hot pursuit,
　　Always stalking your enemies, in hope
　　Of some advantage.
　　And here again, by the seaward tent of Aias,
　　The last on the shore, I see you intently searching
　　The sand for signs, new-made tracks, to tell you
　　Is he here or somewhere else. Your keen scent
　　Is like a Spartan hound's, leading you quickly
　　To its goal.

　　He's just gone in, his face and hands
　　Sweating and bloody from his slaughtering sword.
　　No need to look in now.
　　But tell me, Odysseus,
　　What do you think you're onto? I could help.
ODYSSEUS: Athêna's voice! Dearest of all the gods!
　　Although I can't see you, I can hear you,

And my heart leaps up as a trumpet's call!
Yes, and you've guessed right:
I'm trying to sniff out Aias with his bully shield.
No great friend of mine, to say the least.
Yes, it's Aias I've been tracking all this time.
He did a terrible thing to us last night —
Assuming he's the doer, nothing's certain,
We're all of us at sea over this. So, as usual,
I took it upon myself to seek out the truth.

This morning, we found the cattle we'd plundered from Troy
Hacked to death, slaughtered along with their herdsmen.
It's him, all right: no question there: Aias.
He was seen last night streaking across the plain,
His sword dripping blood. Someone saw him;
And now it's for me to prove it.

These tracks here?
They're his, no doubt about it. As for the others,
They could be anybody's. What to do now?
But I'm glad you've come, lady.
You've guided my course in the past and will again;
And I'll obey.

ATHÊNA: I know, Odysseus; I hurried as fast as I could,
Always eager to guide you in the chase.

ODYSSEUS: Do you mean, dear lady, I'm on his scent?

ATHÊNA: Indeed you are. He's your man.

ODYSSEUS: But why such senseless violence?
What possessed him?

ATHÊNA: Raving jealousy.
Achilleus' armor was given to *you*.

ODYSSEUS: But why take it out on the herds.

ATHÊNA: He thought the blood he was spilling was yours.

ODYSSEUS: Attacking Greeks: is that what he thought?

ATHÊNA: And would have too, if I'd been careless.

ODYSSEUS: Imagine! How did he dare?

ATHÊNA: Night gave him cover — acting alone.

ODYSSEUS: How close did he come?

ATHÊNA: Agamemnon's and Menelaos' tents.

ODYSSEUS: What kept him from murdering them?

ATHÊNA: I did. I called up sickly delusions of triumph
   To thwart his advance and turned his rage on the droves
   Guarded by their herdsmen: sheep and cattle
   Captured from Troy and not yet even sorted.
   Attacking the horned beasts like a madman,
   He cleaved their spines, hacking this way and that,
   Leaving around him a widening circle of death.
   At one moment he thought he held in his grip
   The sons of Atreus, Agamemnon and Menelaos.
   Hacking away at them single-handed;
   At another, he mauled first this general then that.
   I did him one better then, I pushed him headlong
   Toward madness and into my trap.
   When he had finished the slaughter, he bound them together,
   The sheep and oxen that were still alive,
   And marched them back to his tent,
   Thinking they were men, and not horned creatures,
   He has them inside there now, prisoners of war,
   Bound and gagged, torturing them unmercifully.
   But now you'll *see* the man. I'll *show* him.
   Show him in all his rage, his madness.
   And then you'll tell the Greeks!
   Don't worry. The sight won't harm you.
   I'll puzzle his eyes. He won't see you.

   You there! Tormenting your prisoners' limbs!

Come out! I'm calling you, Aias!

Come out in front of your tent.

ODYSSEUS: Athêna! No! Don't call him out here!

ATHÊNA: Quiet! Are you afraid of him?

ODYSSEUS: No, but why bring him out?

ATHÊNA: What's the problem? He's only a man.

ODYSSEUS: Yes, and my enemy — still is.

ATHÊNA: Your enemy's down, Odysseus, enjoy it.

ODYSSEUS: I'd just as soon he stayed inside.

ATHÊNA: Afraid to see a madman?

ODYSSEUS: If he were sane —

ATHÊNA: He won't even see you.

ODYSSEUS: No? He still has eyes.

ATHÊNA: I'll cloud them.

ODYSSEUS: Whatever you say. Gods do what they want.

ATHÊNA: Stay right there. Not a word, now.

ODYSSEUS: I can't say I like it.

ATHÊNA: Aias! You, inside! Can't you hear?

Is this how you treat your ally?

(Aias enters through the large doors of the tent holding a bloody multi-thonged leather whip. He is covered in blood.)

AIAS: Athêna! Zeus' daughter! Welcome!

Thank you for standing by me today!

You'll have a gift of gold from my booty!

An offering for your help in this catch.

ATHÊNA: Thank you.

But tell me now, Aias:

Is your sword well-soaked in Greek blood?

AIAS: Yes, and proud of it I am, too!

ATHÊNA: Have a grand tiff with the Atreus brothers?

AIAS: They won't be slighting Aias again!

ATHÊNA: Dead, are they? Imagine that!

AIAS: Let them try to rob me *now*!

ATHÊNA: Ah, and then there's Laërtês' son.

Did he escape you?

AIAS: The cunning fox?

ATHÊNA: Yes, your rival, Odysseus.

AIAS: Hobbled inside there, dear lady!

Guest of honor, and all that!

He won't be dying anytime soon!

ATHÊNA: You're planning what? What new triumph?

AIAS: Tie him up — to the tent pole, maybe.

ATHÊNA: Ah, poor man! And then what?

AIAS: Whip him to a pulp till he dies!

ATHÊNA: Mercy, Aias! Don't torture him so!

AIAS: Your will is my command, goddess,

In all but this. He dies as I say.

ATHÊNA: Well, if it really means this much,

Do as you like, leave nothing undone.

AIAS: Good! I'm off, then!

But always stand by me,

Just as you did today.

(He enters his tent. The doors close.)

ATHÊNA: You see, Odysseus, the power of the gods?

What man was ever more farsighted

Or better skilled in timely action?

ODYSSEUS: No one I know of. He may be my enemy,

But I still have pity for him, seeing him undone

And yoked to a dreadful fate that could be mine.

We're all of us, every mortal being,

Phantoms and bodiless shadows, smoke in the wind.

ATHÊNA: You must remember your own words, Odysseus.

Never think you're better than the gods.

Never boast of strength or worldly goods.

One day can tip the scale of human events,
Up or down, whatever the gods choose.
We gods love men who think sanely
And hate evil.

(Athêna vanishes. As Odysseus turns to go off, full daylight comes on and music begins as the Chorus of Aias' Sailors from Salamis enters in groups of varying size from the right. Here as elsewhere they speak sometimes individually or in varying combinations.)

*****

from **ANTIGONE** (ca. 442 BCE)

CHARACTERS

Antigone (Antigonê)

Ismene (Ismenê)

[This scene is from the prologue of the play. Antigone is full of anger and grief. She explains to her sister, Ismene, that she wants to disobey her uncle, King Creon's, law. Creon has forbidden the burial and funeral rites for their brother, Polynices. This is a great dishonor in Thebes. Their other brother, Eteocles, was buried with full rites. The two brothers killed each another in a duel for the kingdom of Thebes, leaving Creon, their uncle, to assume the kingship.

Antigone plans on burying Polynices herself, against the law of Creon. She begs Ismene to help her. Ismene refuses.]

Thebes. Barely dawn. The royal palace of King Kreon. ANTIGONÊ leads ISMENÊ from the palace.

ANTIGONÊ: Dear Ismenê, dear sister — we are the last,

       The last in line of the house of Oedipus,

And you would think that we had endured enough

From the ancient curse laid down upon our father.

Is there any suffering that Zeus

Has not used to blight our lives as well?

Both you and I have suffered every evil,

Every pain, every shame, every dishonor.

       But now there's more. They say that *King* Kreon

       Has issued a proclamation, an emergency edict,

To all of Thebes. Have you heard? The evil

That fate once kept for our enemies

Is now used to punish those we love.

ISMENÊ: Heard what, Antigonê? All I've heard,
      All I know is that two sisters lost two brothers
      On a single day at each other's hands;
      And that last night the Argive army
      Fled from Thebes. That's all, I know nothing more,
      Nothing either to cheer me or make me sad.

ANTIGONÊ: I thought as much. It's why I brought you here
      Beyond the gates, so we could talk unheard.

ISMENÊ: What is it? Trouble? I mean, the way you're acting.

ANTIGONÊ: Kreon buried only one of our brothers!
      Eteoklês went to his grave with full rites,
      And well he should, military honors and all,
      A soldier's funeral. His body lies there now,
      Mounded with earth, as the law demands.
      He goes down to death in a blaze of glory.
      The other, Polyneikês, who died a death
      As wretched, he dishonors; proclaiming in Thebes
      That Polyneikês will not be given burial,
      But left lying in the field, unburied, unmourned,
      His body a sweet feast for birds to peck at.

      It's whispered about that Kreon, *worthy* Kreon,
      Made this proclamation for you and me.
      Yes, for me! And he's coming here himself
      To make it clear to anyone who may have missed it.
      No, he's not taking the matter lightly.
      Death is the payment, stoning in the square,
      For anyone who dares to disobey.
      Now it's your turn, Ismenê, to show your colors:
      A loyal friend or traitor to your family.

ISMENÊ: Sister, you're mad! What can I do?

ANTIGONÊ: Decide whether you'll help me or not.

ISMENÊ: Help do what? At what risk?

ANTIGONÊ: To bury him. Help lift his body.

ISMENÊ: Bury? Against the law? Antigonê!

ANTIGONÊ: He's my brother and, yes, yours,
>   However you'd deny it. But no one
>   Will ever say I betrayed my brother.

ISMENÊ: How reckless you are! Defy Kreon?

ANTIGONÊ: Kreon can never make me abandon my family!

ISMENÊ: O sister! Remember how father died!
>   Remember the disgrace he lived with, the hatred
>   People spat at him because of the crimes
>   He himself brought to light! Oh, and his eyes,
>   His eyes ripped out with his own hands!
>   And then mother —
>   His mother and wife in one, who hanged herself
>   With twisted cords once she learned the truth.
>   And last, our two brothers, who killed each other
>   On a single day.
>   We're all alone, Ismenê, the last of our family.
>   Think of the cruel death we'll die, the worst,
>   If we defy the law laid down by the throne,
>   If we question its power. We're only women,
>   It's not our place to fight with men. We're weak,
>   We're ruled by stronger hands; what can we do
>   But submit — not only to this, but to worse?
>   There's nothing I can do, my dear; I'm helpless;
>   And I beg the dead to forgive me if I choose
>   To submit to authority.
>   Hopeless resistance is senseless.

ANTIGONÊ: If that's the way you feel, I wouldn't want you
>   Now to share my labor even if you offered.
>   I will bury my brother; and if I die,
>   I will say that my crime was dear to the gods,
>   And death a glory.

I'll lie beside him I love, and who loved me,

For I choose to please the dead and not the living:

Their demands are longest.

Death is forever. But do as you like, if the gods'

Laws mean nothing to you.

ISMENÊ: They do! But defy the laws of the people?

I'm not that strong, Antigonê; I can't!

ANTIGONÊ: Then that's your excuse.

But I'm going now to bury the brother I love.

ISMENÊ: Oh, Antigonê! I'm so afraid for you!

ANTIGONÊ: Don't be. There's yourself to consider.

ISMENÊ: Keep it quiet, at least! Tell no one!

I'll do the same, I promise!

ANTIGONÊ: No, tell the world if you want!

I'll hate you all the more for your silence!

ISMENÊ: So fiery, when you should be numb with fear!

ANTIGONÊ: I know whom I must please the most.

ISMENÊ: If you can, yes! But you love the impossible!

ANTIGONÊ: I'll fail when I fail — and there's an end.

ISMENÊ: It makes no sense to hunt the impossible.

ANTIGONÊ: If you believe that, then I must hate you,

Hate you as our dead brother will hate you

For the dreadful things you've said.

Leave me my madness. I'm not afraid.

And if I die, I'll die with honor.

ISMENÊ: Go, if you must, but I'll say this:

Rash as your act may be,

You are a deathless friend to those who love you.

*****

from **OEDIPUS THE KING** (ca. 424–421 BCE)

CHARACTERS

> Creon (Kreon)
> Leader
> Oedipus
> Jocasta (Iokastê)
> Attendant

[The play begins as a plague is spreading throughout Thebes. Oedipus, the King of Thebes, is trying to understand the cause of the plague. To do this, Oedipus sends his uncle, Creon, to the Oracle at Delphi for guidance. When Creon returns, he reports what the Oracle has said: there is a murderer in Thebes. When the murderer is caught, the plague will disappear.

Oedipus asks the prophet and seer, Tiresias, who the murderer is. Tiresias responds that it is Oedipus. Tiresias then says that Oedipus has murdered his father and married his mother. Oedipus is shocked and assumes a conspiracy is at work against him. He thinks that Creon is behind the conspiracy. This scene opens as Creon is defending himself against Oedipus's accusation of treason.]

Outside the Palace of Oedipus.

KREON: Men of Thebes — I have heard the accusation
　　　　King Oedipus makes against me, and I have come
　　　In haste, because I'm not a man to endure
　　　Such indignity!

　　　If, in the present crisis,
　　　He believes that I in any way

Intended harm to him in word or deed,
Then I would never choose a long life,
For a life without honor is no life.
This outrage to my name is no small matter.
There is no more grievous charge, none
More heinous than this: to be damned by my own city,
By you, and those closest to me, as a traitor.

LEADER: He spoke in anger, not from careful thought.
KREON: And said that I persuaded the prophet to lie?
LEADER: Yes, but why, I don't know.
KREON: Did he look you straight in the eye?
            Was his mind steady?
LEADER: I can't say.
            I don't judge the deeds of great men.

(OEDIPUS enters from the palace.)

            But here he is now.
OEDIPUS: You, Kreon! You! You have the gall
            To come here! You! You have the audacity
      To approach this house! You who openly plotted
      Its master's murder! You who sought to steal
      My throne, steal my power, like a bandit!
      O by the gods, Kreon, were you so stupid
      To think me a coward, a fool, blind to your plot
      Against me? Did you think I had no eyes
      To see your stealthy moves; that I would not
      Without one moment's pause take arms against them
      In my own defense? What a fool you are, Kreon!
      What a fool! To set out hunting for throne
      And power when throne and power need friends and funds;
      When power and throne are caught with wealth and armies!
KREON: Finished? Then listen to me, I have listened to you,
            And judge on the facts!

OEDIPUS: Ah, Kreon, you have a way with words,
        But how do I listen to a known enemy?
KREON: First things first: listen for a change!
OEDIPUS: First things first, deny that you are a traitor!
KREON: If you think stubborn unreason a virtue,
        Then you are a man who has lost his balance!
OEDIPUS: If you think you can wrong a kinsman
        And escape the penalty, then I tell you
        That *you* are a man who has lost his balance!
KREON: All right! There I agree! Only tell me
        What this wrong is you say that I have done you?
OEDIPUS: Did you or did you not convince me to send
        For that pious fraud of a prophet?
KREON: I did, yes, and I would do it again.
OEDIPUS: How long ago was it that Laïos —
KREON: That Laïos what? I don't understand.
OEDIPUS: Vanished, struck down in his tracks, murdered!
KREON: Years — many long years ago —
OEDIPUS: This prophet — was he practicing then?
KREON: Yes, with the same skill and honor.
OEDIPUS: And what did he say about me at the time?
KREON: Nothing — not while I was about.
OEDIPUS: And you never hunted the king's killer?
KREON: We did, but came away with nothing.
OEDIPUS: Why didn't your prophet accuse me then?
KREON: When I don't know, I prefer to keep silent.
OEDIPUS: But *this* you'd tell, if you were honest.
KREON: What would that be? If I know, I'll tell.
OEDIPUS: If you and he hadn't schemed together,
        He would never have said I murdered Laïos.
KREON: If this is what he said, well then —
        who would know better than you?
    But now it is my turn to question.

OEDIPUS: Ask away. But I'm not a murderer.

KREON: Very well. — Is my sister your wife?

OEDIPUS: Now there's a fact I can't deny.

KREON: And you rule together, equal in power?

OEDIPUS: Everything she wants, she has.

KREON: And I'm the third? We're all of us equal?

OEDIPUS: And that is where you are proven a traitorous friend!

KREON: Not if you see it as I do, rationally.

Why would a man in his right mind ever choose
The distressing cares of kingship over untroubled sleep,
Especially if he has equal power and rank?
Certainly not I. I have never longed to wield
Royal power. Why should I? I live like a king.
Any man with reason would choose as I have.
As it is, I have everything from you.
My life is free. I live unburdened by the demands
Put upon kingship.
But if I were king,
I should be bound to act as a king must act:
Against his will and pleasure. So what could kingship
Give me that I don't have: unruffled power
And influence, without the care, without
The pain, without the threat.
I'm not so insane
Yet to seek out other honors than those
That bring advantage. I'm welcome everywhere.
And those who court your favor, curry mine:
Their success depends on me.
Why give up comfort for worry?
No sane mind is treasonous.
No. I have no leanings in that direction,
And I would never deal with a man who did.
Test me, why don't you? Go to the Pythia at Delphi.

Ask the goddess if I reported correctly.
And if I didn't, if I'm found to be in league
With the prophet, plotting treason, then have me executed!
But not on your vote only; on mine as well:
A double charge. Just don't convict without proof,
on a mere guess.

It is just as wrong to think a bad man good,
As it is a good man bad.
To reject a loyal friend is to tear life
Out of your own breast: there is nothing more precious!
Only time will tell, and time will tell
For certain who is just and who is not;
The traitor is easily spotted.
LEADER: Good advice for a careful man.
       Hasty judgment is often dangerous.
OEDIPUS: Hasty conspiracy is hastily met.
       If I delay, he wins, I lose.
KREON: What do you want? Say it! Banishment?
OEDIPUS: Banishment? No! It is your head I want!
KREON: You refuse to believe! You refuse to yield!

(IOKASTÊ enters from the palace with a woman ATTENDANT and approaches them.)

OEDIPUS: You don't persuade me you're worthy of belief!
KREON: Quite frankly, I think you've lost your wits!
OEDIPUS: In *my* interest, yes!
KREON: And what about mine?
OEDIPUS: But you're a traitor!
KREON: What if you're wrong?
OEDIPUS: But I *must* rule!
KREON: When your rule is evil?
OEDIPUS: Think of the city!

KREON: It is *my* city, too!

LEADER: Please, my lords, no more!

      Look, Iokastê, just in time!

  Let her end this.

IOKASTÊ: Senseless fools! What's all this quarreling in public!

      Aren't you ashamed, stirring up private matters

  When Thebes is sick to the death!

(To OEDIPUS.)

      Come inside, now.

  And you, Kreon, go home.

  Why make something out of nothing?

KREON: Nothing?

      Sister, your husband plans one of two things:

  Either to exile me or to have my head!

OEDIPUS: It's true! I caught him plotting against me!

KREON: No, if I am guilty of anything,

      I will die accursed and consider it a blessing!

IOKASTÊ: Oedipus, I beg of you, believe him!

      In the gods' name, respect his oath,

  Respect me, respect your people!

*****

from **ELECTRA** (ca. 424–421 BCE)

CHARACTERS

Chrysothemis
Electra (Êlektra)
Leader

[In an earlier scene, an old man brings a false report of Orestes' death. In this scene, Electra, Orestes' sister, is grieving over her brother's death. Her sister Chrysothemis tells Electra that their brother Orestes is in fact alive.]

Outside the palace at Mykenê.

CHRYSOTHEMIS: Dear sister! Dear Êlektra! I'm so happy!
      I ran all the way, never thinking how it might look!
    I have news for you! News! Wonderful news!
    An end to your suffering!
ÊLEKTRA: Where would you an end to my suffering?
      My suffering has no cure.
CHRYSOTHEMIS: He's here!
      Orestês is here! Near us now!
    As surely as I stand here in front of you!
ÊLEKTRA: Poor girl, have you lost your mind?
      Laughing at your own sorrows and mine?
CHRYSOTHEMIS: No, I'm not mocking,
      I swear by our father's hearth!
    He's here! Here with us now!
    Among us now!
ÊLEKTRA: Who told you this?
      And you believed him!
CHRYSOTHEMIS: I know what I saw!

My own eyes! I've seen all the proof I need!

ÊLEKTRA: Proof? What proof?

What set you into this feverish whirl?

CHRYSOTHEMIS: Êlektra! Listen! Please!

And when you've heard, then tell me I'm insane.

ÊLEKTRA: Tell me, if it gives you pleasure.

CHRYSOTHEMIS: I'll tell you all I saw.

When I reached father's grave with the offerings I brought,
I saw it running with a newly-poured milk-gift,
And flowers, fresh-cut flowers of all kinds,
Circling the tomb. Amazed, I looked around
For someone nearby. But everything was still.
So I crept to the tomb, and there on its edge I saw
A lock of newly-cut hair, and all at once
My mind flooded with thoughts of him, of Orestês,
Dearest of men, for I knew that there, on that stone,
Lay a token of him!

I took it in my hands, unable to speak,
Tears flooding my eyes. For I knew then,
As I know now, that only you or I
Could have done such a thing, and I knew it wasn't you,
Forbidden as you are from leaving the house
Even to worship the gods, except at your peril;
And I knew it wasn't I. Nor was it mother;
She doesn't like such things; and it could never
Have happened without our knowing.
It can only have been Orestês!
Be brave, my dear! No one's life is fixed
By unchanging fortune; and ours has seen bad days.
But perhaps today will lead to a better life.

ÊLEKTRA: Ah, what a fool you are! I pity you.

CHRYSOTHEMIS: What are you saying, Êlektra?

How can this not please you?

ÊLEKTRA: You know nothing.

You're lost in some dream-world.

CHRYSOTHEMIS: Dream-world? I know what I saw!

ÊLEKTRA: He's dead, poor girl. Orestês is dead.

Your hopes in *that* are dashed.

No use looking to him for help.

CHRYSOTHEMIS: Who told you such a thing?

ÊLEKTRA: A man —

A man who was there when he died.

CHRYSOTHEMIS: I don't believe it!

Where is he? Where?

ÊLEKTRA: There. In the palace.

A welcome guest for our mother.

CHRYSOTHEMIS: Oh, no. But the offerings

— On the grave — where did they come from?

ÊLEKTRA: From someone to honor Orestês' death.

CHRYSOTHEMIS: Dear god will this never end?

I ran here bursting with joy at my news,

Knowing nothing, nothing, of what has happened,

Only to find new sorrows.

ÊLEKTRA: Now you understand.

Just do as I say and we can lighten

This load of sorrows.

CHRYSOTHEMIS: Bring the dead to life?

But how is that possible?

ÊLEKTRA: That's not what I said.

I'm not a fool.

CHRYSOTHEMIS: If I have the strength, I'll do it.

ÊLEKTRA: Then have the courage to do as I say.

CHRYSOTHEMIS: I'll do anything I can to help.

ÊLEKTRA: Just be prepared for a hard fight.

CHRYSOTHEMIS: I know. I'll do all I can.

ÊLEKTRA: All right, then, here's my plan.

As you know, we haven't a friend left here,
None to stand by, to help us, everyone dead.
We're alone now, sister, just the two of us.
As long as I knew Orestês was still alive,
I cherished the hope that he would return to Argos
To avenge our father's murder.
But now Orestês is dead.

I now turn to you for help, Chrysothemis,
To help your sister slay our father's murderer:
To slay Aigisthos.
There. No more secrets.

But what must it take, what, to make you act
Before you stop doing nothing? Hope is dead.
What hope can you still cling to? All that's left
Is grief for a lost treasure, grief for years
Wasted without a husband, no marriage, no bridal songs,
Nor any prospect, ever, to get these things.
Aigisthos is no fool. Can you imagine
He'd ever allow children of yours or mine
To grow to strength and threaten his precious safety?

But do as I say, my dear, and you'll have the thanks
Of the dead below the earth, our father and brother.
You'll be free, free as you once were born,
Free to marry nobly. Don't you see?
You'd win respect for yourself, for me, if only
You'll do as I say.

What citizen of Argos, what stranger,
Will see us and not greet us with words of praise?

"Here, friends," they'll say, "here are two sisters
Who rescued their father's royal house!
They faced a triumphant enemy, they risked their lives,
They avenged bloody injustice! They deserve our love,
Deserve our respect. Let them be honored at festivals
And public assemblies for their great heart and courage."
That's what they'll say, and in life and death our fame
Will never fade.

Dear sister, listen to me!
Take up our father's cause!
Take up our brother's!
Share their pain!
Free me! Free yourself!
Free us of this disgrace!
A life of dishonor dishonors the noble mind!
LEADER: Be careful, my dears.
        Caution is best: both for those
    Who speak and those who listen.
CHRYSOTHEMIS: Caution? Yes.
        She'd have done well to do so.
    But she's out of her mind:
    Arming herself in rashness
    And calling on me to help.

You're a woman, Êlektra. You're weak.
You don't have the strength to fight your enemies.
Their fortune grows daily by leaps and bounds,
While ours fails, withering away to nothing.
Who could plot to kill a man like Aigisthos
And escape unscathed? He'll punish us with miseries
Worse than we suffer already if we're discovered.
What good is fame and honor if we end up dead?

But worse even than that is to long for death
And not be allowed to die.

Please, Êlektra, before we destroy ourselves
And our whole family, rein in your anger.
Everything you've said I'll keep a secret
As though you never spoke it. You must learn,
However late, to yield to those in power
When you are helpless.

LEADER: Do as she says.
      Caution and common sense
Are the best life offers.

ÊLEKTRA: I can't say I'm surprised.
      I knew you'd refuse. All right.
      I'll do it alone. It can't be left untried.

CHRYSOTHEMIS: O god, if only your mind had been so set
      On the day father was murdered!
      But you did nothing!

ÊLEKTRA: The will was there, just not the understanding.

CHRYSOTHEMIS: Then keep that understanding all your life.

ÊLEKTRA: This lecture of yours tells me you refuse to help.

CHRYSOTHEMIS: Yes, because to act is to court disaster!

ÊLEKTRA: I envy your caution; it's your cowardice I hate!

CHRYSOTHEMIS: The day will come, when you'll see I was right.

ÊLEKTRA: No, sister, that day will never come.

CHRYSOTHEMIS: The future's a long time; we'll wait and see.

ÊLEKTRA: Get out of here! Out! You're useless to me!

CHRYSOTHEMIS: I could be useful, but you refuse to learn.

ÊLEKTRA: Go on, then, go! Go tell it to your mother!

CHRYSOTHEMIS: No, my dear, how could I hate you so!

ÊLEKTRA: Then think of the hurt you're doing me, the dishonor!

CHRYSOTHEMIS: Hurt? Dishonor? I'm trying to save you.

ÊLEKTRA: To be saved, must I accept your view of justice?

CHRYSOTHEMIS: Yes, till you've come to your senses.

ÊLEKTRA: How clever you are, and to be so wrong.

CHRYSOTHEMIS: Yes, you describe your problem exactly.

ÊLEKTRA: Are you saying I don't have right on my side?

CHRYSOTHEMIS: Being right can sometimes bring disaster.

ÊLEKTRA: No, I refuse to live by laws like that!

CHRYSOTHEMIS: If you do this thing, you'll see I was right.

ÊLEKTRA: I *will*, *will* do it! You can't frighten me!

CHRYSOTHEMIS: You can't be stopped, then? Nothing will change you?

ÊLEKTRA: No! There's nothing worse than wrong thinking!

CHRYSOTHEMIS: Nothing I say makes any impression on you.

ÊLEKTRA: I made up my mind on this long ago.

CHRYSOTHEMIS: What more can I say? I'll go.
 You refuse to listen, and I can't accept
Your choice of action.

ÊLEKTRA: Then go. I won't come
 Trailing after you,
 However much you wish it.
You're chasing illusions;
What can be more foolish?

CHRYSOTHEMIS: Think yourself right, if you must.
 When trouble come, you'll think back on my words —
But too late.

*****

from **OEDIPUS AT COLONUS** (ca. 406 BCE)

CHARACTERS

Oedipus
Leader
Chorus
Messenger
Antigone (Antigonê)
Ismene (Ismenê)
Theseus (Thêseus)

[After years of exile, Oedipus goes to Athens to see the king, Theseus. Oedipus is with his daughter, Antigone. Antigone's sister, Ismene, joins them later.

Years earlier, the Oracle of Apollo told Oedipus that he would die in Athens. So Oedipus has come to Athens to spend the last moments of his life. In the scene that follows, Oedipus feels his impending death. He is ultimately carried away to die in a hidden, isolated place.]

The Sacred Grove of the Eumenides.

OEDIPUS: Children!

Come!
Follow me!
A strange marvel has come to pass.

I am now *your* guide who once was led by you.

(Both daughters reach out to help him, a movement he senses unseen.)

No! Do not touch me!

I alone will discover the sacred grave
Which Fate has destined for my burial ground.

(He beckons to them again.)

    This way! Come! O come!
Hermes leads me, Guide of the Dead,
And Persephonê Queen of the Underworld!

(He begins a slow progress towards the Sacred Grove.)

    O light I do not see!
Sunlight that once was mine!
I feel you one last time!
Warm this ragged body
As I go to close my life
In the dark house of Death.

(Turning to THÊSEUS.)

    And you, truest of friends,
Be blest, you and your land
And all of your people,
And in your days of greatness to come,
Remember me in my death,
The seed of all your fortune
In time to come,
Ever renewing,
Forever new!

(OEDIPUS turns upstage once more toward the Sacred Grove and goes slowly straight into its center in the direction of the skênê, the Brazen-Floored Threshold of Earth, whose doors open slowly to admit him. He is followed at a distance by ANTIGONÊ and ISMENÊ, THÊSEUS behind them, and behind him an ATTENDANT. When all have entered, the CHORUS reassembles.)

LEADER:

> Goddess! Unseen Persephonê! If it is lawful,
> let me honor you with my prayers!
> And you, Ruler of Eternal Night!

CHORUS:

> > Hear me!
> > Aïdoneüs!
> > Aïdoneüs!

LEADER:

> Grant our friend an easy passage—

CHORUS:

> > free of pain,
> > unlamented,
> > to the dark land below,
> > > fields of the dead,
> > > all-enshrouding,
> > to the Stygian house!

LEADER:

> Uncounted sorrows came to him without cause.
> I pray that some just god will exalt him in glory.

CHORUS:

> Daughters of Earth! Daughters of Darkness!
> > And you, dread
> > beast, unconquered,
> > ever-watchful
> > at the gates of many guests,
> > snarling at the cavern's jaws,
> > guardian of Hades' hall
> > as legend says —

LEADER:

> — and you, Death, son of Tartaros and Gaia,
> restrain the beast and make the passage clear
> as our friend approaches the endless Fields of the Dead!

CHORUS:

> On you I call,
> god of eternal sleep,
> lead him gently —
> give him rest —

(No movement. Then a MESSENGER enters through the doorway of the skênê and comes forward into the orchestra.)

MESSENGER: Oh, my fellow citizens, to tell you simply
  Would be to say that Oedipus is dead.
  But more has happened than can be simply said,
  Or said in few words.

LEADER: He's dead, then, poor man?
MESSENGER: I assure you. He's passed from life.
LEADER: How? By god's grace painless?
MESSENGER: This is the very thing that's such a wonder.
  You know, you saw it, how he left here,
  Led by no friend, himself leading the way.
  Wel l— when he had come to the steep descent,
  The Brazen-Floored Threshold of Earth that leads
  To the earth's roots, he paused at one of the many
  Branching paths, near the rocky basin that marks
  The covenant of Thêseus and Perithoüs.
  And there, midway between the hallowed basin
  And the Rock of Thorikos, with its hollow pear tree
  And marble tomb, he sat down and undid
  His filthy garments.

  He then called to his daughters
  To fetch him fresh water from the stream nearby,
  To wash himself and pour libations to the gods.
  We watched them climb the Hill of Dêmêter, goddess

Of green things and growth, and soon return
With the water to wash and dress him as custom requires.
When everything was done according to his pleasure,
And none of his commands were left undone,
Zeus of the Depths made the earth moan
With subterranean thunder.

Frightened, the girls trembled and fell to their knees
Beside their father and wept inconsolably,
Beating their breasts and wailing. And when he heard
The piteous sound, he folded his arms around them,
And said: "Children: this day is your father's last.
All that I once was is no more,
And the burden that you bore of caring for me
Is lifted now. It has not been easy, my children;
That much I know. And yet, one word frees you
Of all your pain and grief: that word is Love.
Never will you know greater love
Than you have had from me.
Go now, and live the rest of life without me."

And so, clinging together, the three of them wept.
And when they ended, and no more was heard,
There was a silence, and from that silence, suddenly,
A voice cried out that stood our hair on end
In panic fear! The god called him — called him
Again and again, echoing all about us,
Urging him on with shouting: "Oedipus! Oedipus!
It's time! You stay too long!"

Knowing it was the god's voice, he asked
Thêseus to come and said: "Dear friend,
Give me your right hand as a solemn pledge

To my children; and you, children, give yours to him.
Swear to me that you will never betray them,
Never of your own will, but promise in kindness
Always to do what is best for them."
And to his friend Thêseus he swore —
As befits a king, and not giving way to grief —
That he would do as asked.

This done,
Oedipus reached his sightless hands to feel
For his daughters and said: "Children, prove yourselves
Noble and brave, and leave here, never asking
To see what law forbids, nor hear what must not
Be heard. Go quickly now. Only King Thêseus,
Whose right it is, may witness the mystery
That now begins."

This much we heard him say,
And came away, sobbing, with the girls.
But then a moment later we turned around —
And the old man was nowhere to be seen,
Only Thêseus, his hands before his face,
Shading his eyes as against some dreaded sight
So terrible as not to be endured.
And then, quickly, with no word spoken,
We see him bow in reverence, with a prayer
To earth and the gods above.

In what manner Oedipus passed from life,
No mortal man but one can tell: only Thêseus.
It was no fiery bolt from god, no whirlwind
Sweeping in from the sea that took him off;
But either some guide came from the gods,

Or the earth below opened its unlit doors
In love to receive him.

Whatever way, his passage
Was free of all lament, sickness, and pain:
If ever any mortal's end was wondrous,
His surely was.
If what I say sounds foolish,
Believe what you like.
I can say no more.

*****

Sophocles

THE READING ROOM

YOUNG ACTORS AND THEIR TEACHERS

Adkins, A. W. H. *Merit and Responsibility: A Study in Greek Values*. Oxford: Oxford University Press, 1960.

Bieber, Margarete. *The History of the Greek and Roman Theater*. 2nd ed. Revised. Princeton, N.J.: Princeton University Press, 1961.

Blundell, Sue. *Women in Ancient Greece*. London: British Museum Press, 1995.

Bowra, C. M. *Sophoclean Tragedy*. Oxford: Oxford University Press, 1944.

Brown, A. L. *Sophocles: Antigone*. Warminster, England: Aris and Phillips, 1987.

Burkert, Walter. *Greek Religion*. Cambridge, Mass.: Harvard University Press, 1985.

Bury, J. B., and Russell Meiggs. *A History of Greece to the Death of Alexander the Great*. 4th ed. Revised. New York: St. Martin's Press, 1991.

Davies, M. *Sophocles: Women of Trachis*. Oxford: Oxford University Press, 1991.

Dawe, R. D. *Sophocles: Oedipus the King*. Cambridge: Cambridge University Press, 1982.

Easterling, P. E., ed. *Sophocles: Women of Trachis*. Cambridge: Cambridge University Press, 1982.

Ehrenberg, Victor. *Sophocles and Pericles*. Oxford: Oxford University Press, 1954.

This extensive bibliography lists books about the playwright according to whom the books might be of interest. If you would like to research further something that interests you in the text, lists of references, sources cited, and editions used in this book are found in this section.

Finley, M. I. *The Ancient Greeks: An Introduction to Their Life and Thought.* New York: The Viking Press, 1964.

Guthrie, W. K. C. *The Greeks and Their Gods.* London: Methuen, 1950.

Jones, John. *On Aristotle and Greek Tragedy.* Stanford, Calif.: Stanford University Press, 1980.

Kells, J. H. *Sophocles: Electra.* Cambridge: Cambridge University Press, 1973.

Kirkwood, G. M. *A Study of Sophoclean Drama.* Ithaca, N.Y.: Cornell University Press, 1958.

Lattimore, Richmond. *The Poetry of Greek Tragedy.* Baltimore, Md.: The Johns Hopkins University Press, 1958.

_____. *The Story Patterns in Greek Tragedy.* Ann Arbor: The University of Michigan Press, 1964.

Lesky, Albin. *Greek Tragedy.* London: Ernest Benn, 1978.

Neils, Jenifer. *Goddess and Polis: The Panathenaic Festival in Ancient Athens.* Princeton, N.J.: Princeton University Press, 1992.

Rehm, Rush. *The Greek Tragic Theatre.* London and New York: Routledge, 1992.

Reinhardt, Karl. *Sophocles.* Oxford: Blackwell, 1979.

Segal, Erich. *Oxford Essays in Greek Tragedy.* Oxford: Oxford University Press, 1984.

Slater, Philip. *The Glory of Hera.* Boston: Beacon Press, 1968.

Stanford, W. B. *Sophocles: Ajax.* New York: St. Martin's Press, 1963.

Steiner, George. *Antigones.* Oxford: Oxford University Press, 1984.

Traulos, Johannes. *Pictorial Dictionary of Ancient Athens.* London: Thames and Hudson, 1971.

Ussher, R. G. *Sophocles: Philoctetes.* Warminster, England: Aris and Phillips, 1990.

Vernant, Jean-Pierre, and Pierre Vidal-Naquet, eds. *Myth and Tragedy in Ancient Greece.* New York: Zone Books, 1990.

Vickers, Brian. *Towards Greek Tragedy.* London: Longman, 1973.

Webster, T. B. L. *Sophocles: Philoctetes.* Cambridge: Cambridge University Press, 1970.

Whitlock, Blundell M. *Helping Friends and Harming Enemies: a Study of Sophocles and Greek Ethics.* Cambridge and New York: Cambridge University Press, 1989.

SCHOLARS, STUDENTS, PROFESSORS

Aristotle. *The Poetics.* By Gerald Else. Ann Arbor: University of Michigan Press, 1967.

Barker, Ernest. *The Politics of Aristotle.* Oxford: Oxford University Press, 1946.

Boesche, Roger. *The Theories of Tyranny from Plato to Arendt.* University Park: The Pennsylvania State University Press, 1996.

Easterling, P. E., ed. *The Cambridge Companion to Greek Tragedy.* Cambridge: Cambridge University Press, 1997.

Goldhill, Simon. *Reading Greek Tragedy.* Cambridge: Cambridge University Press, 1986.

Gombrich, Ernst. *Art and Illusion.* London: Phaidon, 1977.

Hall, Edith. *Inventing the Barbarian: Greek Self-definition through Tragedy.* Oxford: Oxford University Press, 1989.

Hogan, James C. *A Commentary on the Plays of Sophocles.* Carbondale and Edwardsville: Southern Illinois University Press, 1991.

Hornblower, Simon, and Antony Spawforth, eds. *The Oxford Classical Dictionary.* 3rd ed. Oxford: Oxford University Press, 1996.

Jung, Carl Gustav, and Carl Kerényi. *Essays on a Science of Mythology: The Myth of the Divine Child and the Mysteries of Eleusis.* Bollingen Series XXII. Princeton, N.J.: Princeton University Press, 1969.

Just, Roger. *Women in Athenian Law and Life.* London and New York: Routledge, 1991.

Keuls, Eva C. *The Reign of the Phallus: Sexual Politics in Ancient Athens.* Berkeley and Los Angeles: The University of California Press, 1993.

Kitto, H. D. F. *Form and Meaning in Drama: A Study of Six Greek Plays and of Hamlet.* 2nd ed. London: Methuen, 1964; New York: Barnes and Noble, 1968.

_____. *Greek Tragedy: A Literary Study.* 2nd ed. New York: Doubleday, 1964; 3rd ed. London: Methuen, 1966.

_____. *Poiesis: Structure and Thought.* Berkeley and Los Angeles: The University of California Press, 1966.

Knox, Bernard. *Word and Action: Essays on the Ancient Theater.* Baltimore, Md. and London: The Johns Hopkins University Press, 1979.

Kott, Jan. *The Eating of the Gods: An Interpretation of Greek Tragedy.* New York: Random House, 1973.

Lax, Batya Casper. *Elektra: A Gender Sensitive Study of the Plays Based on the Myth*. North Carolina and London: McFarland and Company, Inc, 1995.

Lloyd-Jones, Hugh. *The Justice of Zeus*. Sather Gate Lectures, Vol. 41. Berkeley and Los Angeles: The University of California Press, 1971.

Lonsdale, Stephen H. *Dance and Ritual Play in Greek Religion*. Baltimore, Md.: The Johns Hopkins University Press, 1993.

Meier, Christian. *The Greek Discovery of Politics*. Cambridge. Mass.: Harvard University Press, 1993.

_____. *The Political Art of Greek Tragedy*. Baltimore, Md.: The Johns Hopkins University Press, 1993.

Murray, Gilbert. *Five Stages of Greek Religion*. New York: Columbia University Press, 1925.

Neumann, Erich. *The Great Mother: An Analysis of the Archetype*. 2nd ed. Bollingen Series XLVII. New York: Pantheon Books, 1963.

_____. *The Origins and History of Consciousness*. 2nd ed., printing corrected and amended. Bollingen Series XVII. New York: Pantheon Books, 1964.

Nietzsche, Friedrich. *The Birth of Tragedy and Other Writings*. Cambridge Texts in the History of Philosophy. Cambridge: Cambridge University Press, 1999.

Page, Denys L. *Actors' Interpolations in Greek Tragedy*. Oxford: The Clarendon Press, 1934.

Pickard-Cambridge, A. W. *Dithyramb, Tragedy and Comedy*. 2nd ed. Revised by T. B. L. Webster. Oxford: Oxford University Press, 1962.

_____. *The Theatre of Dionysus in Athens*. Oxford: The Clarendon Press, 1968.

Pomeroy, S. *Goddesses, Whores, Wives, and Slaves: Women in Classical Antiquity*. New York: Shocken, 1995.

Ringer, Mark. *Electra and the Empty Urn: Metatheater and Role Playing in Sophocles*. Chapel Hill and London: University of North Carolina Press, 1998.

Roberts, Patrick. *The Psychology of Tragic Drama*. Boston and London: Routledge and Kegan Paul, 1975.

Rosenmeyer, Thomas G. *The Masks of Tragedy*. Austin: The University of Texas, 1963.

Seaford, Richard. *Reciprocity and Ritual; Homer and Tragedy in the Developing City State*. Oxford: Oxford University Press, 1994.

Segal, Charles. *Tragedy and Civilization: An Interpretation of Sophocles.* Cambridge: Harvard University Press, 1981.

_____. *Oedipus Tyrannus. Tragic Heroism and the Limits of Knowledge.* Oxford: Oxford University Press, 1993.

_____. *Sophocles' Tragic World: Divinity, Nature, Society.* Cambridge: Harvard University Press, 1995.

Sutton, D. F. *The Greek Satyr Play.* Meisenheim am Glan, Germany: Hain, 1980.

Taplin, Oliver. *Comic Angels and Other Approaches to Greek Drama through Vase-Paintings.* Oxford: Oxford University Press, 1993

Thucydides. *The Peloponnesian Wars.* Translated by Rex Warner. Harmondsworth, England: Penguin Classics, 1972.

Turner, Victor. *The Forest of Symbols.* Ithaca, N.Y: Cornell University Press, 1973.

_____. *Dramas, Fields, and Metaphors.* Ithaca, N.Y: Cornell University Press, 1974.

Vernant, Jean-Pierre. *Myth and Thought among the Greeks.* London and Boston: Routledge and Kegan Paul, 1983.

Wilamowitz, T. von. *Die dramatische Technik des Sophocles.* Berlin: Weidmann, 1917.

Winkler, John. *The Constraints of Desire: The Anthropology of Sex and Gender in Ancient Greece.* New York and London: Routledge, 1990.

Zeitlin, Froma I. *Playing the Other: Gender and Society in Classical Greek Literature.* Chicago: University of Chicago Press, 1996.

THEATERS, PRODUCERS

Bartsch, S. *Actors in the Audience.* Cambridge and London: Harvard University Press, 1994.

Bennett, Simon. M. D. *Mind and Madness in Ancient Greece.* Ithaca, N.Y: Cornell University Press, 1978.

Forrest, W. G. *The Emergence of Greek Democracy.* New York: McGraw-Hill, 1966.

Garkand, Robert. *The Greek Way of Life.* Ithaca, N.Y.: Cornell University Press, 1990.

Georgiades, Thrasybulos. *Greek Music, Verse and Dance.* New York: Da Capo Press, 1973.

Jaeger, Werner. *Paideia: The Ideals of Greek Culture.* 3 vols. New York: Oxford University Press, 1945.

Kolb, Frank. *Agora und Theater.* Berlin: Gebrüder Mann, 1981.

Ley, Graham. *A Short Introduction to the Ancient Greek Theater.* Chicago: The University of Chicago Press, 1991.

Parke, H. W. *Festivals of the Athenians.* Ithaca, N.Y: Cornell University Press, 1977.

Sourvinou-Inwood, Christine. *Reading Greek Culture: Texts and Images, Rituals and Myths.* Oxford: Oxford University Press, 1991.

Steiner, George. *The Death of Tragedy.* New York: Alfred A. Knopf, 1961.

Vernant, Jean-Pierre. *Myth and Society in Ancient Greece.* New York: Zone Books, 1990.

Wiles, David. *Tragedy in Athens.* Cambridge and New York: Cambridge University Press, 1997.

Winkler, John J., and Froma I. Zeitlin, eds. *Nothing to Do With Dionysos? Athenian Drama in Its Social Context.* Princeton, N.J.: Princeton University Press, 1992.

ACTORS, DIRECTORS, PROFESSIONALS

Arnott, Peter. *Greek Scenic Conventions in the Fifth Century B.C.* Oxford: Oxford University Press, 1962.

_____. *Public and Performance in the Greek Theatre.* London: Routledge, 1989.

Aylen, Leo. *The Greek Theater.* Rutherford, N.J.: Fairleigh Dickinson University Press, 1985.

Bain, David. *Actors and Audience: a Study of Asides and Related Conventions in Greek Drama.* Oxford: Oxford University Press, 1977.

_____. *Masters, Servants, and Orders in Greek Tragedy: Some Aspects of Dramatic Technique and Convention.* Manchester, England: Manchester University Press, 1981.

Buxton, R. G. *Persuasion in Greek Tragedy.* Cambridge: Cambridge University Press, 1982.

Cooper, Lane. *The Greek Genius and Its Influence.* New Haven, Conn.: Yale University Press, 1917.

Csapo, Eric, and William J. Slater. *The Context of Ancient Drama.* Ann Arbor: The University of Michigan Press, 1995.

Dodds, E. R. *The Greeks and the Irrational*. Berkeley and Los Angeles: University of California Press, 1951.

Earp, F. R. *The Style of Sophocles*. Cambridge: Harvard University Press, 1944.

Else, Gerald F. *The Origin and Early Form of Greek Tragedy*. Martin Classical Lectures, vol. 20. Cambridge, Mass.: Harvard University Press, 1965.

Fergusson, Francis. *The Idea of Theater: A Study of Ten Plays, The Art of Drama in Changing Perspective*. Princeton, N.J.: Princeton University Press; London: Oxford University Press, 1949.

Flickinger, R. C. *The Greek Theater and Its Drama*. Chicago: University of Chicago Press, 1936.

Green, J. R. *Theatre in Ancient Greek Society*. London and New York: Routledge, 1994.

Green, J. R., and E. Handley. *Images of the Greek Theatre*. Austin: University of Texas Press, 1995.

Halperin, David M. *One Hundred Years of Homosexuality*. New York and London: Routledge, 1990.

Herington, C. J. *Poetry into Drama: Early Tragedy and the Greek Poetic Tradition*. Berkeley and Los Angeles: The University of California Press, 1985.

Hornby, Richard. *Script into Performance*. Austin: University of Texas Press, 1977.

Knox, Bernard M. *The Heroic Temper*. Berkeley: The University of California Press, 1964.

Mastronarde, D. *Contact and Disunity: Some Conventions of Speech and Action on the Greek Tragic Stage*. Berkeley and Los Angeles: The University of California Press, 1979.

Taplin, Oliver. *Greek Tragedy in Action*. Los Angeles: The University of California Press; London: Methuen, 1978.

Walcot, Peter. *Greek Drama in Its Theatrical and Social Context*. Cardiff: The University of Wales Press, 1976.

Walton, J. Michael. *Greek Theatre Practice*. Westport, Conn. and London: Greenwood Press, 1980.

_____. *The Greek Sense of Theatre: Tragedy Reviewed*. London and New York: Methuen, 1984.

THE EDITIONS OF SOPHOCLES' WORKS USED
FOR THIS BOOK

Sophokles. *The Complete Plays*. Translated by Carl R. Mueller and Anna Krajewska-Wieczorek. Hanover: Smith and Kraus, 2000.

SOURCES CITED IN THIS BOOK

Hornblower, Simon, and Antony Spawforth, eds. *The Oxford Classical Dictionary*. New York and Oxford: Oxford University press, 1996.

Knox, Bernard. *Oedipus at Thebes*. New Haven, Conn.: Yale University Press, 1998.

Moore, John (intro., transl.), David Grene (ed., intro.) and Lattimore Richmond (ed.). *Sophocles II: Ajax, The Women of Trachis, Electra & Philoctetes*. Chicago: University of Chicago Press, 1969.

Pickard-Cambridge, A. W. *The Dramatic Festivals of Athens*. 2nd ed. Revised by John Gould and D. M. Lewis. Oxford: The Clarendon Press, 1968.

Segal, Charles. *Interpreting Greek Tragedy: Myth, Poetry, Text*. Ithaca, N.Y.: Cornell University Press, 1986.

Watling, E. *The Theban Plays*. New York: Penguin Classics, 2003.

Whitman, Cedric H. *Sophocles: A Study of Heroic Humanism*. Cambridge, Mass.: Harvard University Press, 1951.

Awards

"And the winner is . . . "

YEAR BCE	DIONYSIA FESTIVAL IN ATHENS	LENAEA FESTIVAL IN ATHENS
ca 534	Thespis *Unknown title*	
484	Aeschylus *Unknown title*	
476	Phrynichus *Phoenissae*	
468	**Sophocles** ***Triptolemus***	
ca 467	Aeschylus *Seven Against Thebes*	
ca 463	Aeschylus *Danaid trilogy*	
ca 459	Aeschylus *Suppliant Women*	
ca 458	Aeschylus *Oresteia*	
455	Euripides *Daughters of Pelias* (third prize)	
447	**Sophocles** ***Unknown title***	
442	A prize is institutionalized and first awarded to the best comic actor at the City Dionysia. (unknown recipient)	
441	Euripides *Unknown title*	
ca 439	**Sophocles** ***Unknown title*** **(first prize)** Euripides *Alcestis* (second prize)	
431	Euphorion (son of Aeschylus) *Unknown title* (first prize) **Sophocles** ***Unknown title*** **(second prize)** Euripides *Medea, Philoctetes, Dictys, Theristae* (third prize)	

428	Euripides *Hippolytus*	
427		Aristophanes *Banqueters* (second prize)
426	Aristophanes *Babylonians*	
425		Aristophanes *Acharnians*
424		Aristophanes *Knights*
423	Aristophanes *Clouds I* (third prize out of three)	
422		Aristophanes *Proagon* (first prize) Aristophanes *Wasps* (second prize)
421	Aristophanes *Peace I* (second prize)	
415	Xenocles *Oedipus, Lycaun, Bacchae,* *Athamas* (first prize) Euripides *Trojan Women, Alexandrus, Palamedes, Sisyphus* (second prize)	
414	Aristophanes *Birds* (second prize)	
410	Euripides *Phoenician Women* (second prize)	
409	**Sophocles** ***Philoctetes***	
ca 405	Euripides *Bacchae* (posthumously produced)	Aristophanes *Frogs*
401	**Sophocles** ***Oedipus at Colonus*** **(posthumously produced)**	
387	Aristophanes *Cocolus*	
321	Menander *Anger*	

Unknown title = play lost

First prize unless otherwise specified

Aristophanes won prizes in the comedy genre; the others won in the tragedy genre.

INDEX

The entries in the index include highlights from the main In an Hour essay portion of the book.

ABOUT THE AUTHOR

Carl Mueller was a professor in the Department of Theater at the University of California, Los Angeles, from 1967 until his death in 2008. There he directed and taught theater history, criticism, dramatic literature, and playwriting. He was educated at Northwestern University, where he received a B.S. in English. After work in graduate English at the University of California, Berkeley, he received his M.A. in Playwriting at UCLA, where he also completed his Ph.D. in Theater History and Criticism. In 1960–1961 he was a Fulbright Scholar in Berlin.

A translator for more than forty years, he translated and published works by Büchner, Brecht, Wedekind, Hauptmann, Hofmannsthal, and Hebbel, to name a few. His published translation of von Horváth's *Tales from the Vienna Woods* was given its London West End premiere in July 1999. For Smith and Kraus he translated individual volumes of plays by Schnitzler, Strindberg, Pirandello, Kleist, and Wedekind. His translation of Goethe's *Faust Part One* and *Part Two* appeared in 2004. He also translated for Smith and Kraus *Sophokles: The Complete Plays* (2000), a two-volume *Aeschylus: The Complete Plays* (2002), and a four-volume *Euripides: The Complete Plays* (2005). His translations have been performed in every English-speaking country and have appeared on BBC-TV.

Smith and Kraus wishes to acknowledge Dr. Susan Ford Wiltshire, Professor of Classics, Emerita, Vanderbilt University. She was immensely helpful with the spellings of Greek names and places.

We thank Hugh Denard, whose enlightened permissions policy reflects an understanding that copyright law is intended to both protect the rights of creators of intellectual property as well as to encourage its use for the public good.

Know the playwright, love the play.

Open a new door to theater study, performance, and audience satisfaction with these Playwrights In an Hour titles.

ANCIENT GREEK

Aeschylus   Aristophanes   Euripides   Sophocles

RENAISSANCE

William Shakespeare

MODERN

Anton Chekhov   Noël Coward   Lorraine Hansberry
Henrik Ibsen   Arthur Miller   Molière   Eugene O'Neill
Arthur Schnitzler   George Bernard Shaw   August Strindberg
Frank Wedekind   Oscar Wilde   Thornton Wilder
Tennessee Williams

CONTEMPORARY

Edward Albee   Alan Ayckbourn   Samuel Beckett
Theresa Rebeck   Sarah Ruhl   Sam Shepard   Tom Stoppard
August Wilson

To purchase or for more information
visit our web site inanhourbooks.com